Ada & Eddie

A Novel

T0349386

Also by the Author

Amanita Virosa: The Destroying Angel
Roundfire Books, ISBN: 978-1-80341-681-6

A harrowing tale of the unwavering defiance of a group of people who galvanise a mini revolution in and around North London in the early nineties. Loosely based on actual events engendering the climate of the eighties and nineties and the devious politics practised by certain Whitehall government officials, a motley cast of ordinary citizens embarks on a dangerous mission to change the status quo. As an evocative thriller, the plot's twists and hair-pin turns will keep you anxiously flipping pages to uncover the truth, culminating in an unforgettable grand finale.

Ada & Eddie

A Novel

Barry Harden

ROUNDFIRE
BOOKS

London, UK
Washington, DC, USA

CollectiveInk

First published by Roundfire Books, 2025
Roundfire Books is an imprint of Collective Ink Ltd.,
Unit 11, Shepperton House, 89 Shepperton Road, London, N1 3DF
office@collectiveinkbooks.com
www.collectiveinkbooks.com
www.roundfire-books.com

For distributor details and how to order please visit the 'Ordering' section on our website.

Text copyright: Barry Harden 2023

ISBN: 978 1 80341 701 1
978 1 80341 707 3 (ebook)
Library of Congress Control Number: 2023949048

A CIP catalogue record for this book is available from the British Library.

Design: Lapiz Digital Services

UK: Printed and bound by CPI Group (UK) Ltd, Croydon, CR0 4YY
Printed in North America by CPI GPS partners

We operate a distinctive and ethical publishing philosophy in all areas of our business, from our global network of authors to production and worldwide distribution.

To Isabel

Chapter 1

Seeing a body lying face down in the grass far from any road or track can only suggest one of two things: spontaneous death or murder. So coming across such an occurrence, what would anyone do?

One would most probably call the police, don't you think? The problem with that was that the nearest town was around thirty miles away and the nearest road was about seven and there was no phone anywhere around that I knew of. I didn't own a mobile and I still don't. I've never wanted one. What would have been the point? Who would I call? I didn't know anyone, and no one knew me. Besides, even if there was a public phone box, I doubt that I would have been able to figure out how to use it. So there you are, and that's the truth of it all.

If I had walked the thirty miles or so to a police station, supposing that I knew where one might be found, it would have jeopardised my whole existence. It would have knocked me right off the course that I had chosen to follow. My desire had been to stay alone for as long as I could, to remain there in my place, my little wilderness which I had adopted as my home. I hadn't wanted any contact with the world, but there I was, suddenly confronted by a dead person.

There was no way that I could just walk off and leave the body, was there? The crows were bound to peck away at it as they do with the other dead things that I've seen, and it's so disgusting because they always start on the eyes. There were no trees nor hedges around there to speak of nor anywhere else close by where I could have secreted the body away from their sight. So, what could I have done?

It suddenly occurred to me—why was this person dead, and was it possible that I might be the next one to die having discovered this poor lifeless soul? Let's face it. The killer might still be out there watching, maybe coming back to inspect the body and then seeing me, think that I had seen him kill this poor dead thing! And then what? Kill me with a gun or a knife, or just beat me to death? Then there would be two of us having our bits pecked by crows.

But I had to know first and foremost, I just had to find out why this person in front of me was dead. Truthfully, I didn't really have a clue as to what I should have done next. I mean, think about it. Anyone confronted with that situation is going to need a few minutes to think things through.

It was difficult. I had been on my own since I was fifteen, and then out of the blue, there I was standing over another human being, a dead one at that. I'm telling you—it was a very curious and most unpleasant feeling. It was as if I feared contact with another person. But as I looked at her lying there, her long, black hair caked with dried mud, all I wanted to do was touch her, turn her over and look into her face. I guessed from her figure that she was at least twenty years younger than me, thirty-something or maybe a bit less. Her shoulders were slumped forward, and her left leg was turned inwards in an awkward position. God, how I wanted her to breathe just to stop the torment that was gradually building up inside my head!

***

Dusk was forming across the moor. The waning sun had cast long shadows along the clumps of tall grasses and thistles, massed armies of feathered plumes. I loved that time of the day, the secret time when rabbits and hares darted out from their hiding places under the rocks and from the beds of dried-out nettles. Wisps of mist slowly slithered over the moor and whirled like phantoms rising into nothingness as the flutter of the night owls' and harriers' wings swept over the copses in search of some unsuspecting prey.

And then I did it. I touched her hair! The dew was already beginning to fall, and I could feel it cold and sharp on my fingers. I sat down beside her. Dare I turn her over? Dare I look into her face? That was the closest I had been to another human being for quite some time. It was exciting, I admit, exhilarating in a strange and scary sort of way. I took a deep breath and then carefully, slowly, I turned her over. I remember that she was surprisingly heavy to lift. I worried that I might have defiled her beautiful young skin with my grubby, calloused hands.

It took all of my strength to lift her just enough to roll her onto her back. I could feel the softness of her contours against me as I rolled her over, my left hand on her shoulder and my right against her hip. At last, I could see her.

When I think back on it, I still weep, just as I did then. I couldn't stop. Never, not for years and years had I dared to look so closely into another human's face. I sat there staring down at her until the cloaks of darkness fell and overshadowed our surroundings so that it was just her and me under the moon's spotlight.

In retrospect, the night was not really that cold. Early September can often be like that, misleading, one night frosty and the next warm but with ghosts of deathly cold air causing one to shudder. I couldn't leave her alone, not lying there like that on the bare damp ground. I gathered up a bundle of dry grass to make a pillow for her head, and I covered her body with my old, dingy blanket. Then I settled down beside her. I don't know why, but I slipped my hand beneath the blanket to hold hers. She was cold, her fingers stiff. I felt sure that I could warm her, breathe some tiny flicker of life back into her corpse. But she didn't move. She stayed cold and silent ... and dead.

A fox barked in the distance and a fieldmouse squealed as it found itself victim to a weasel or stoat. As usual, I rested my body that night but not my senses.

***

In the morning, I took time to examine my companion. Her complexion had paled and greyed and the skin on her face had slightly pulled back. There was no sign of blood, but I could see the dull bruises encircling her wrists and ankles. I turned her head, which lolled to the side as if detached, and I realised that her neck had been broken.

She had been wearing mascara when she was murdered. Black rivulets had trickled down and dried on either side of her nose. It was not right! Tagged upon a dead thistle, I could see some rabbit fur still wet with dew. It was enough to clean her face, and then I could really see her. She was beautiful, and I would have done anything to bring her back to life, to see her eyes see me, hear her voice ask me who I was or where she was or even hear her scream. But there was nothing I could do except to hold her close to me and stroke her hair and cheeks. She was dead. I knew it, but she was now in my care, for me to look after her and tend to her deathliness.

There was a cave so well hidden that no one else knew of it. I had discovered it while searching for mushrooms the previous year before the shooting started. When the weather was bad, I would sometimes spend days hidden away in there, but I was always careful to leave no tracks. It was my secret place, nobody else's, and I thought she could stay there where no one would ever find her.

She wasn't very heavy, probably between eight and nine stone, but being dead made her feel a lot heavier. It took me two whole nights to carry her across the rough ground to my hideaway. At my age, things never get easier. Once inside, I gathered a bouquet of wild mint for her which grew down by the riverside. I placed a sprig of heather in her hand, but of course, she couldn't hold it and it fell to the ground just to remind me that she was actually, decidedly dead. She looked so radiant in the chink of light that beamed down onto her face from the early morning sun. I can see her now and feel a kind of anguish in remembering. Why did they have to do that to her ... break her neck? Why?

It occurred to me that I was falling in love with her, a strange thing to say, I know, but for the first time in my life, I felt that I had a kind of relationship with another person, even though it was a dead one. It was the closest contact that I had experienced in an awfully long time except for my love of an old cat that had been my companion for a few years. I had called him Tom, but one night, he disappeared just as he had arrived, quite unexpectedly. I love cats, but he was really something special to me. I still miss not seeing him even after all this time. I suppose he must be dead by now. He probably got caught up in a snare or was poisoned, something like that. I'm sure he didn't really want to go.

Nearly a week had passed since I found her, and the cave was beginning to take on a not-so-pleasant odour. Her perfume had faded, and her clothes had become dank from the dampness of my blanket and from the floor of the cave. Besides all that, corpses tend to leak quite seriously after a short while, and it was then that I realised the time had come for me to bury her body. I had seen the bodies of animals blow up with gas and knew the smell of her decaying body would eventually attract the attention of something or somebody if I didn't get her below the earth soon. The idea of not seeing her again was a loss I would have to bear but it was something I had to do if only to stop others from interfering with her.

The cave was on the edge of what I thought of as my domain. It was on a low hillside hidden by rocks and brambles, and below it ran a fast-flowing but shallow river. I had often washed in the waters, cleaned my clothes on sunny days, and gathered fruit and nuts from the wild plum, apple and hazel trees, or mushrooms. I always got by until the first chilly days of October, and then I would find shelter in or near a more accommodating source of food. I never went hungry, not the kind of desperate hunger that some people have had to endure.

To the east along the riverbank was a farmhouse with a barn and a couple of smaller outhouses. I had always kept my distance. Not once had I seen any activity there and always assumed that it was derelict. I had been tempted to investigate the place, but I always withdrew at the last minute, mainly because it was none of my business prying into things that didn't concern me. It was like keeping that other world away. Difficult to explain, really. It was a sort of mistrust of the other side of things. Now I had to do something, though not for myself but for my beautiful companion. Death had been claiming her in every conceivable way. I needed tools to bury her: a shovel, a gardening fork, and maybe something to carry her away in, just to make the job a little bit easier.

The door to the main barn at the farm was partially missing, so I knew I could come and go as I wished without making the slightest sound. It was afternoon, sunny, but with plenty of cover along the river edge for me to reach the property unseen. I waited for ten minutes before making my move. Confirming that there was no one around, I slipped in through the barn door. I could see what I needed despite the darkness except for some kind of transport, but I thought that could wait for the moment. I wouldn't need it until her grave was finally dug.

I wanted to find a good place to bury my beloved, somewhere where the earth would neither flood nor be too stony. Somewhere dry with a view of the sky and the river. Somewhere she could hear the birds sing during the day or hear the owls hooting at night. A place where she could smell the scent of the wild mint cast up by the river whenever a fox brushed against its leaves. It needed to be somewhere as close to paradise as it could possibly be. Somewhere as beautiful as she.

After some time, I found the very place beneath a cluster of old coppiced ash trees, sheltered from the weather but in full view of the sky and of all the beauties of the riverside. I checked the soil. It was perfect but it would take me a few days to dig a grave large enough and fitting enough for my lovely dead companion.

I hurried back to the cave to rest until nightfall and to explain to my dearest what I was about to do for her. She remained silent, as she would, but in my mind, it was easy for me to imagine that she was really listening and knew that I cared.

Her odour was becoming overpowering. That night, I decided to sleep with my head at the entrance to the cave where the air still retained some of its fragrance. Even the mosquitoes stayed away, but that was to be expected, wasn't it?

Chapter 2

Being alone is one thing, but thinking that one is alone when there is someone else out there is a different matter altogether.

It took me the best part of four nights to dig the grave. Each night before dawn, I returned to the barn with the shovel and gardening fork that I had borrowed, replacing them just as they were when I had found them. But it was on the fourth night, just as I was leaving, that my escape was interrupted.

She stood there in the half-light with her pitchfork pressed against my chest. I hadn't even heard her arrive or seen her until I walked straight into its prongs.

'Care to tell me what you're doing here?'

I was at a loss as to what to say. I gripped my cap so hard that I felt my fingernails digging into the palms of my hands, right through the canvas. 'I don't want any trouble, ma'am. I didn't know anyone was here. All I wanted was to borrow some tools so I could do some digging ... vegetable plot, you know.'

'Come on, nobody digs a vegetable garden in the middle of the night, not unless they're mental.' She paused for an explanation that never came. 'So, what's your name? Who are you?'

I tried to remember some of the names that were used when I was a child before my parents were killed or what I was called by the staff at the orphanage. It came to me none too soon. 'Edward Dew,' I stuttered. 'That's the name I remember being called when I was a kid. But not so long ago, I used to be called Tom by most people. That's when I had my old tomcat and after I ran away, but I suppose it would be best if it were Eddie. I'm used to being called that, you see.'

She lowered the implement but still held on to it. 'Okay, Eddie it is. Now, what have you been up to, Eddie? I've been watching you through my telescope for a long time, and it's clear you've been up to something. I can tell you're about to do some burying. That's what it looks like to me.'

It was an odd declaration, for sure. I'd been in that part of the moor since the late spring that year. In past years, when winter was approaching, I'd take myself off to one of the hostels for the homeless and then leave again when the weather perked up. But ever since I'd been up on the moors from spring through autumn for the past five or six years, I had chosen to be alone, finding some derelict cabin or a haystack in which to pass the nights until it got really cold and food became scarce. It was much easier on my mind to be alone, unbothered with questions that I didn't really want to answer. Now there I was, caught by a woman who seemed strangely calm and didn't chase me off on the end of her pitchfork.

Of course, I said nothing. She continued, 'From watching you, I've got a feeling that whatever it is you're doing, you're getting yourself into very serious trouble.'

I was stunned that I had been discovered so easily. For forty years, from fifteen to middle age, what I prefer to call midden age, I had lived without any company to speak of, without ever having been caught like that. If I had been a bit younger, I might have run for it, but this woman posed no threat to me and seemed to know more about me than I thought she should have done. If she had been watching me that closely, had she seen me having a wee or bathing, for example? When you're alone and you think no one's about, then you do these things without thinking or the least embarrassment. Now I wondered just how much she had seen.

'Ma'am, I swear I mean no harm. I try to stay away from people and not cause any trouble for anybody. I hadn't seen anyone 'round here, so I thought this place was abandoned. I'm really sorry I trespassed on your property, missus. Can I go now?'

I must've looked harmless to her, maybe even pathetic. 'I tell you what,' she said as she leaned her pitchfork against the remnant of the barn door. 'You must be hungry seeing as you've been out there digging since dusk yesterday. Come with me. I'll get you something to eat.'

I followed her into the farmhouse, through the kitchen door, into a dimly lit, sparsely furnished room. 'Have a seat,' she muttered as she heated a tea kettle and gathered some crockery and cutlery. 'Don't say a lot, do you?'

'Sorry, missus, but I got a lot on my mind.'

She placed a couple of plates, two mugs and a teapot hiding under a cosy on the table. 'Got some bread, cheese and tomatoes you can have with your tea. By the way, my name's Ada, so you can stop calling me missus. Now tell me, what're you doing out here? If you're going to drink my tea and eat my tomatoes, you'll have to give me something more than your name, unless you want me to think of you as a bagman, but I prefer not to insult you in that way.'

I thought for a moment, dismayed that my status could actually be reduced to bagman. I struggled with an answer to her question. What she was really asking me was, did I want to give up the secret of my cave, but then having been found out, I realised that there was no way I could keep the secret and admit at the same time to the existence of the young woman. I decided to trust Ada. She seemed sincere enough.

'Well, it's that I found a body up there on the moor, right in the middle of my patch, you know, the part where I roam about, and I don't know how she got there. She was murdered, that's for sure, and I've been looking after her in my cave for the last week, but she's not looking so good nor smelling quite as she did when I found her. So, I figured that I needed to bury her.'

'Eddie, what on earth were you thinking? If she's been murdered, then the police should hear about it. She's probably got a family out there desperately waiting for news of her. What if she's got children or a family who depend on her? It must be reported at once.'

'But how do I explain that she's in my cave? They'll think that I killed her and that I tried to hide her. Then they'll take her away, and I won't know where she is anymore.'

Ada looked quite troubled by that and not a little perplexed. 'Why is that so important to you, Eddie? Do you know who she is?'

'No, I've never seen her before.'

'So, why will it trouble you if you don't know where the police will take her?'

'Because she's mine. I found her and we sit together, like company. Just her and me.'

'But you were going to bury her, weren't you? You wouldn't see her again anyway.'

'No, no! That's different, you see. I could still talk to her, know where she is, visit her, bring her flowers.'

'Eddie, for heaven's sakes, she's dead! You must let her go!'

We both sat in silence as I thought about Ada's advice. Deep down, I knew she was right, but I needed time to think it through. After a long pause, she continued. 'Eddie, you've spent far too much time outdoors alone, and it seems to me that you've lost your senses.'

'Maybe you're right, Miss Ada. She's the first human being I've ever gotten close to, even if she is dead. She's alone, like me, and somebody needs to care for her, even if it's just to remember her and bring her flowers. She's so young and someone hated her enough to kill her and throw her away like she was rubbish. I need a little time to think about it.

'Thank you, Miss Ada, for the tea and sandwich. Very kind of you but I must be going. I'm sure you've got things to do.' I rose to leave.

'You know, Eddie, I've been watching you ever since you arrived up there in the spring. It pains me to see a human being

11

scavenging about the bushes looking for food. Why don't you stop by for lunch while you're around. I don't know how you can tell the time without a watch, but any time between noon and two o'clock would be fine.'

'That's very nice of you to offer, missus. I haven't had a proper meal in months since I left the homeless shelter. Is it okay if I stop by tomorrow?'

'Of course you can, Eddie. And while you're out there, think about doing the right thing with the dead girl.'

'I will, Miss Ada. Thank you again.'

For the next few days, I stopped by for lunch with Ada. She was kind-hearted but also seemed to be strong-willed and independent and the type of person who kept her cards close to her chest. Ada looked to be in her mid-fifties, robust, of medium height and build with drawn-back greying hair and stern green eyes. A bit odd, she liked to wear a hat indoors as well as out. When she was indoors, she kept her gloves under her hat so that she wouldn't forget where they were. At least, that's what she told me.

We had long, interesting conversations over lunch and got to know a bit more about each other. Ada told me that she was a widow and her husband, George, had died unexpectedly, but she didn't say how and I didn't pry. She and her husband apparently had strong opinions about the government and politicians. I just listened whenever she brought it up as I didn't know enough to hold a conversation or have my own opinions about that sort of thing. But I kept getting the feeling that she wasn't telling me everything and I thought it best not to meddle.

I told Ada about my parents having been killed in a car accident and how devastated I was when my brother and I were separated. I never saw my brother again and didn't have a clue how to find him. I told her about how people's cruelty had led me to a life of solitude and my attachment to innocent animals. They, too, know the struggle to live in an unkind world. She seemed to appreciate that and though we came from different lives, we seemed to have a few things in common.

One day over lunch, Ada said to me in a serious tone, 'Eddie, I have a proposition for you which I hope you'll consider. Neither you nor I are getting any younger and I thought maybe we could help each other out. I could really use some help around the farm: chopping wood for the fire, gathering vegetables, doing repairs around the house, that sort of thing. I could also use some company, and you and I seem to get along alright. Would you like to live here with me and help out in exchange for room and board? I have an extra bedroom in the back you can have with a nice fireplace. What do you think?'

A comfy bed with a mattress, home-cooked meals, warm nights sleeping in front of a fire, Ada's companionship. I moved in the next day.

I decided to boldly ask her, 'Missus, can I have a cat to live here with us as well?'

She looked at me sternly. 'We shall see ... and for Christ's sakes, stop calling me missus!'

***

She made me take a bath, cut my long, knotted hair, which I can tell you took her an awfully long time, and shaved off my beard. That took a long time, too. Despite the towel, I felt almost naked. I saw what remained of my trousers sticking out of her waste bin. When she saw that I had noticed them there, she laughed. 'I suppose I should really compost those, shouldn't I?'

I kept quiet, fearing the worst, wondering if she was going to deprive me of clothes, you know, be a prisoner, a naked slave. I'd been told about that sort of thing when I was a kid just to frighten us at the home. I was so relieved when she pushed a box of men's clothes towards me. 'Don't worry,' she said, 'they're perfectly clean. They belonged to my late husband, George.'

The clothes fit fine for the moment, though the trousers were a bit short. The shoes were at least one size too small but in better shape than the old plimsol and my cut-down wellington boot. I had to cut it down because it made my leg sweat something terrible, and then my leg would start to itch and scratching made it even worse. I wore George's shoes when I had to but otherwise went around the house in my socks. I couldn't recall the last time that I'd had the luxury of a pair of underpants or a proper vest, so it didn't bother me that there weren't any to be had for now.

***

The morning had passed without me hardly noticing as she showed me around her land and the outhouses. Eventually, she went back into the kitchen and called out that she was going to prepare some lunch for us.

'Let's see what's on the news and find out if the weather is going to hold up a bit longer,' she called out as she fiddled with her old wireless.

'...will take place at Canterbury Cathedral on the 23rd. In other news, it has just been reported that the police will soon call off the search for the thirty-two-year-old female courier who went missing from her home in Portsmouth on August 15. Friends and employers of Marina Penrith are anxious to hear from her and hope that she is safe and well. Any information as to her whereabouts or sightings of her would be welcomed by Portsmouth Constabulary.'

Ada suddenly turned off the radio. 'Eddie, how do you know that the young lady you found was murdered?'

'There were bruises on her wrists and ankles and her neck was broken. Can we go up to check on her after we've eaten, make sure she's still there?'

'Yes, Eddie, but then we need to go to town. You did hear the man on the wireless, didn't you?'

'Yes, but Portsmouth is miles from here. Funny that it's near to where I come from. It's just along the coast to Southampton. How on earth would we ever get there?'

'There's a Constable Coggins who lives just this side of Castleton. He'll know what to do. But let me do the talking. Otherwise, you might find yourself in prison. You know, what you've done with that poor girl was very considerate but might appear to the authorities as if you were an accessory to her murder. God, what have I gotten myself into! Can you ride a bike, Eddie?'

***

I never realised how fast one could travel on a tandem bicycle until that day. Some years ago, I had found an old bike with no tyres in a hedge near Manchester, and though it made my backside a bit sore. I had learned to ride quite well and only fell over four or five times. I thought that was quite good, but one night, a van passed me, knocked me over, and ran over the bicycle, so that was that. I should have had some lights, I suppose, but such luxuries were out of my range.

Ada was so full of energy and did most of the work, especially on the hilly parts. My problem was the shoes. Pushing on the pedals was a bit painful, but eventually my feet went numb though I was still able to do some of my share. It took us an hour and a half to reach the constable's cottage.

He was asleep in a chair outside the front door when we arrived. It was only the click of the garden gate that brought him out of his slumber.

'What can I do for you?' he grumbled as he sat up straight in his chair.

'My friend here found a woman's body on the moors while he was camping in this fine weather. He didn't want to leave her where she was in case she was preyed upon by the crows and wild things, so he carried her down to a cave. He thinks that she's been murdered.'

There was a pause as our astounding revelation sunk in. 'Murdered, you say? How do you know? Where did he find the body? And damn it, can't he speak for himself? You turn up here out of the blue, not so much as a phone call, and tell me that you've got a body! It's bloody Thursday afternoon, nearly teatime, and you say there's been a murder. I'm going to be up all night over this! Can't you come back tomorrow morning or better still ... Oh, for God's sakes, just give me the details. Names?'

'Ada Gampe with an *e* on the end, and he's Edward Dew.'

'Right, so he found a body. Where exactly on the moor?'

'He can show you.'

With the tandem sticking out of the back of the police Range Rover, the three of us eventually arrived at the moor just as dusk was falling and the autumn mist was starting to rise.

'There's not a lot here, is there? Not much to go on, don't you know? So, where's the body?'

It was quite dark when we eventually reached the cave, and even with the torchlight, the policeman was unable to reach any conclusions.

Back at the house, Ada made a pot of tea, and by 8.30 pm, Constable Coggins was back on the road to Castleton, probably quite happy to be on his way home.

Chapter 3

Not long after sunrise, there was a sharp knock at the door. Ada opened it and in spilled four men—two in uniform, one in a suit and another without any kind of dress sense whatsoever.

'Constable Coggins tells us that you have a female murder victim stashed away in a cave. Is that correct?' demanded the latter in an aggressive manner.

'Yes,' replied Ada.

'Do you know whose body it is?' he continued in the same tone of voice.

'Yes,' I said. 'She's mine!'

The four policemen looked at each other cynically. Ada gave me an irritated glare and slowly shook her head. 'What he means is that he found her on the moor and carried her to a cave to prevent wild things from feasting on her.'

The shabby detective became even more hostile. 'Well, that was thoughtful, wasn't it? Probably destroyed all the evidence. In fact, it sounds a bit fishy to me as if he was trying to hide her, which makes you two prime suspects. So, who are you? I'm going to have to caution you that the constable here will take your statements. First, let's take a look at the body and get her transferred to the mortuary, and then we'll see where he claims to have found her.'

I led the way to the cave where Detective Decrepit, that's what I called him, peered through the opening at the body of the young victim. 'God help us,' he gasped as he quickly turned away in disgust. 'The stench alone is sickening!'

The second detective took a deep breath and carefully crawled in through the entrance to the cave, shining his torch right onto the decomposed face. He'd hardly been in there a minute before he started to gag. 'It's her, the young woman from Portsmouth. Help me out of here, will you!'

Afterwards, I took them up onto the moor, to the spot where I had found her. 'How do you know that it was here?' asked Decrepit, looking at me suspiciously.

'Because he knows what he's doing,' Ada snapped. 'I don't know what's the matter with you, but you seem to have a nasty chip on your shoulder. Why don't you treat him with some respect? After all, he's trying to help you.'

The detective turned on her as if he wanted to hit her and probably would have done if the other one had not stood in his way. The second detective calmly asked me, 'How exactly was she lying? Can you show us?'

I got down on my hands and knees and flopped face down onto the turf. I tried to twist my leg into the contorted position I had seen her in, but to no avail. 'I can't do the awkward bit,' I said. 'My leg's too stiff.'

They all looked at me for some time, lying there pretending to be dead before Ada demanded, 'Can he get up now? Give him a hand!' The mean detective backed off and left his assistant and one of the constables to get me up on my feet again.

'She was lying right here, just as I showed you, but with her leg in a funny position. You can see where the grass is still flat as it hasn't rained since I moved her.'

'You know a lot about all this stuff, don't you?' the mean one muttered under his breath. I thought to myself, there's something funny about this man. He didn't seem to be a very happy person. Ada put her arm round me and assured me that I was doing all right.

The younger detective and one of the two uniformed men studied the ground, carefully walking in ever-larger circles until the constable called out, 'Looks like some oil here and some marks from a vehicle of some kind, wheels close together. Quadbike, I should think.'

Decrepit shouted back, 'Leave the thinking to us, Constable. It's not your job to think!'

'Sorry, Sergeant Wragge. I was just trying to be helpful.'

Now that was a coincidence. Some years have passed since my last visit to a police station. I was picked up one night on a charge of vagrancy, then showered off, given some clean clothes, and held until I saw the magistrate the following morning. While I was in the police cell, I heard some of the policemen laughing about how a Sergeant Wragge had run off with a fellow officer's wife and that he was suspected of wrecking a drug bust case by leaking to the pusher's family details of an imminent arrest. When the pusher was finally caught, Sergeant Wragge pretended to have a bad back for a year, and the case was thrown out for lack of a witness. I wondered whether this was the same man. He didn't have a north country accent, not like the others. I whispered to Ada, 'Ask him where he comes from.'

She looked at me with a smile. Directing herself to Sergeant Wragge, she asked, 'Where are you from? Listening to your accent, you're not from around here, are you?'

'None of your bloody business!' came the terse reply.

The second constable sidled up beside her and cautiously whispered, 'He's up from Sussex. Hastings, I think. He's a bit rough around the edges, so don't take it personally.'

Wragge shot a glance at Ada and flicked his cigarette butt. 'Book them for aiding and abetting!' he commanded his assistant.

'Can't do that, Sergeant. There's no evidence of them having committed a crime. The sooner we pass this over to the Hampshire CID, the better. All we can do is send them the information that we've gathered here today and let them handle it.'

***

It was lunchtime when we all got back to the farmhouse. An ambulance and two forensics officers were waiting. The two constables led the way back to the cave, leaving Wragge and his assistant at the farmhouse. Ada invited them in for a cup of tea in the kitchen. Wragge took out a cigarette from behind his right ear and proceeded to light it.

'Sorry, Sergeant Wragge, but I don't allow smoking in my house.' Indignantly, he stomped to the kitchen sink and threw the cigarette into the washing up bowl.

'My God, have you no respect for people's property? Heaven help anybody who's banged up with you!'

If looks could kill, Wragge would have been six feet under. He stormed out of the kitchen only to return within a second, grabbed a cup of tea from the table and marched off once more, spilling it down his scruffy outfit. Finally, plonking the cup down on a box in the yard, he hurried off to catch up with the forensics team, leaving the other detective to drink his tea in peace.

'My name is Detective Constable Richards. I think you've made an enemy of my sergeant and he's not a man to be gainsaid. He will do his best to get you into court as accessories to murder. I think your best chance is to tell me all that you know so if worst comes to worst, I can help you in your defence.' He sat down at the kitchen table, produced a notebook and pen, and started to write. 'Who found the body, when, and what time of day was it?'

I told him it was me and that little more than a week had passed since I found her. He was a bit shocked at that.

'Why didn't you report it earlier?'

'I couldn't. I had no means of transport and no phone. It was only by chance that Ada caught me in her barn and she took me to see Constable Coggins. We got to his place on her tandem.'

He turned to Ada. 'Is this true? You only just met him?'

'Yes, that's right. He'd been living rough in the moor and looks out for the animals there. If he finds a lost sheep, he'll take it back to its fold and I've seen him climb a tree to return a fallen nestling to its nest. I'd been watching him, but only from a distance.'

I hadn't realised that she knew so much about me. But she was right, though. I did what I could. I hate to see any animal in distress, and there were quite a lot of them up there, I can tell you. It's incredible the lengths that some people go to in the name of countryside preservation. It seems to me that they would be happier if there was no countryside to preserve at all.

'Eddie lives at my farmhouse now.' Ada continued. 'He's helping me with odd jobs in exchange for a warm place to stay, especially now with winter on its way.'

Richards wrote it all down. 'Look, you'll get a visit within a day or two from some other police officers. Tell them all this and anything else you can think of that might be of significance. Did you hear any kind of vehicle at any time? That would give us a better idea as to how long she might have been there.'

'Oh, she hadn't been there hardly any time at all,' Eddie said. 'She was still loose. You know, the stiffness wasn't there. I saw that she had been tied hand and foot and that her neck was broken. Who could do that to her? She was so lovely. I turned her over to see if there was any life in her, but she was dead. But I didn't hear anything. There'd been a hard wind across the moor that day and sometimes it blows the sound away.' I thought that might help to explain why I didn't hear anything. And I was right.

'Good, now that is useful. Which day was it and about what time?'

'Well, what day is it today?' I asked.

'Thursday,' Ada volunteered.

'Then today, four days, three days ... that's eight add one, that's nine. Nine days ago at about six, no, seven o'clock because dusk fell not long after I found her. Goodness, that's quite a long time, isn't it?'

'So, you've had her up in the cave all this time? No wonder there's a bit of an odour, to put it mildly.'

'Well, it's better than having the animals take her apart. Have you ever seen how quickly foxes and badgers can dispose of a corpse? And as for wild boar ... well, I've seen deer and goats stripped down to nothing in just two to three days, not that I've seen any boar around here. There'd be nothing left but a couple of snags of skin. It takes absolutely no time at all. That must be why they, whoever killed her, left her up here. She is the woman from Portsmouth, isn't she? We heard it on the radio this morning. Has she got any family?'

He seemed pleased with what I had said.

'I'll pass this on to the other policemen who will visit you soon. I can't tell you much about the family, only that she was a divorcee for three years and her married name was Penrith, Marina Penrith.'

'What was her surname before that?' I asked.

'It's probably a coincidence, but it was Dew, same as you. Originally, she came from Southampton after having arrived with her father from Australia. She then moved to Portsmouth when she was about twenty-five.'

'I come from Southampton, too! I ran away from my orphanage when I was in my early teens and have tried to keep my head down ever since. I was separated from my twin brother after some years. That was towards the end of the fifties. He was sent off to Australia while I was kept at the home. That's why I'm always trying to keep out of sight, and now here I am up to my neck in a murder enquiry. I'm sorry, Ada. I think you must have found me on the wrong day.'

Richards finished writing and stood up. 'I'd better go now. Look, I'm going to try to find out more about her family. If I find any connection between you, I'll let you know. But this really does need to be your secret for the time being. Don't mention it to anybody else under any circumstances. Wragge would most likely use it against you. Just watch out for him. He's a particularly nasty piece of work.'

With that, Richards left us to join his colleagues. The scene was eventually cleared. Only a ribbon surrounding the cave remained, and after checking that Marina Penrith was no longer there, we returned to the farmhouse.

We sat in silence for a while, deep in thought, until Ada stood and announced that she was going to bed. She gave me a hug and said, 'Don't worry. It'll be all right in the end.'

There was a lot for me to think about that evening. It struck me as a little odd that the young woman and I had the same name. Is that why I felt so attached to her and didn't want to let her go? Was she the daughter of my twin brother, and if so, where was he? All these thoughts kept tumbling into my head until I could see the dim silhouettes of the trees heralding the beginning of another day. It was only then that I finally fell asleep.

Chapter 4

No one came to see us the following day, giving me a little more time to adjust to the loss of my young, deceased companion. I grieved for her, strange as it may seem, but finding her, even though she was dead, had such a profound effect on me. I hadn't given a lot of thought as to who might have killed her or why she was killed. I'd been too busy making a home for her and me, and now that she was gone, I had a dreadful emptiness that even now saddens me when I think about her.

Ada was organised about everything. She could sort out any situation, and to prove it, she began by asking me about important documents.

'So, you've got no birth certificate, no national insurance number, not even a medical card. Actually, Eddie, there is nothing to say that you exist and no evidence that you did not fall onto the moors from the sky either. Well, that's not a good start, is it? So you're Edward Dew, and that's all we have.'

'At the orphanage, I used to be called Little Eddie by nearly everybody except one Scottish teacher who jumbled it up and called me "laddie".'

'Edward, didn't you know that the Scottish call boys "laddie"? They're the same with girls except they refer to them as lassies.'

I saw that Ada was laughing to herself. 'Is that funny, Ada?' I asked, slightly puzzled.

'No, not at all, Eddie,' she answered while pulling the corners of her mouth downwards with her right thumb and forefinger. 'Let's move on. What was your twin brother's name?'

'Ernest. We used to call him Ernie. I never knew what happened to him. They separated us when we were about six or seven years old. He was sent off to Australia on some sort of government scheme. I remember him crying and being dragged away and that was the last I ever saw of him. The awful thing is that I can't even remember what he looked like. Probably a bit like me, I suppose, us being twins.'

'You can be quite lucid at times, can't you, Edward?' she said smiling.

'I prefer Eddie.' I reminded her, 'That's who I really am inside.'

'I'm sorry about that,' she said, and her apology sounded quite sincere. 'Well,' she continued, 'can you recall the orphanage at all? Where in Southampton might it have been? Have you any clear picture of it?'

'It must have been somewhere near a rubbish tip because after I ran away, I joined up with some other kids and we collected all sorts of stuff: some bits of food chucked out from local shops, empty bottles, and so on, all from the tip. That was when you could get a penny for an empty beer bottle at the off-licence. Some of the kids used to pinch empties from outside the back of one shop and got money back when they returned them to another shop. They all got caught eventually.

'I don't have many good memories of those days. I never had a chance even to see where my parents were buried. That's not very good, is it? I wonder what happened to Ernie. You know, Ada, this is the first time that I have ever tried to go back to those days. Nobody has ever asked me anything about myself before. No one's been interested. When you've been on your own for as long as I have, all this comes as a bit of a surprise. If it hadn't been for poor, young Marina, I would've never met you. Strange, isn't it? It all seems to have a purpose. I wonder where this is going to lead us, that is, if you still want me to stay here.'

'Yeah, we'll get along just fine,' she said. 'Don't you worry about that.'

I began to relax a little more in her company. I suppose it was while I was thinking over those bits of my childhood that it suddenly struck me.

'Ada, there was a large, black stone cross outside the orphanage, and someone had scratched into it, "Be damned if you enter here." I couldn't read it properly at the time but all us kids were threatened with the stick if we were caught writing on anything other than an exercise book.'

'Good, we're starting to get somewhere now. Give it some time. Then we can see about getting you some proper identity.'

***

Another day had passed before two policemen from Portsmouth appeared. They had stayed at Castleton overnight, acquainted themselves with the details of our involvement in the case and were, at first, rather overbearing. Ada didn't like that at all.

'If you're going to be rude, I suggest you go back to Portsmouth. Without an arrest warrant, you won't even get a cup of tea here let alone any explanation as to how Edward found the young woman.'

I could see that they were stung by her words and looked rather sheepishly at one another. Ada continued, 'If we are to help you at all, it's for you to tell us as much as you can about her. When Edward found her on the moor, there was nothing to suggest how she got there. So what about her family? That would be a good place for you to start.'

In a monotone voice, the older detective muttered, 'She had been married, divorced three years ago, both parents dead. Mother, Hilda, died from cancer five years since and her father, Ernest, was the victim of a fatal hit-and-run four months ago. Otherwise, there are no other relatives from what we can tell. The company she worked for as a courier offered a reward for information regarding her whereabouts, but we don't know where that stands now that she's no longer with us.'

The news about Ernest was a real shock. I began to think that the coincidences were all part of a strange plot. But I couldn't see any point in it. And were they really part of me? My head was spinning, and I struggled to put those questions aside for now.

'I suppose we'd better go out to inspect what evidence remains,' said the policeman with the same bored tone. We all returned to the two sites where the detectives shuffled around without saying much.

Ada put her arm round me. 'Are you alright, Eddie? It's not certain, is it? It might not be your brother after all, and she might not have been your niece.' Ada had a real compassion in her face, as if she was trying to shield me from what we both knew was beginning to form a distinct shape.

'Excuse me!' I shouted to the two men. 'Excuse me, but how old was her father when he was killed?'

The reply was staggering. 'He was born in 1950. Unfortunate family, I'd say. His parents were killed in a bomb blast, one of Hitler's bombs hidden away under their garage. That was always a big problem after the war. People built sheds and garages over unexploded bombs, and then one day, the whole lot goes up. It looks like the end of the line for that family. None left that we could find.'

I turned around and looked into Ada's face. It was as much as I could do not to break down. She gently squeezed my hand. 'It's okay, Eddie. Don't fret, love.'

The whole thing seemed overwhelming and my thoughts were becoming muddled. In the course of a couple of weeks, I had gone from being a loner living on the moor without any real focus beyond the next meal to a man mourning a family I had never known and living with a woman on whom I had come to rely. It was the kind of sick feeling that a nice cup of tea was unlikely to ever cure.

I suppose an hour had passed until one of the men, I can't remember which, called out that they were finished up on the moor, and we started the trek down to the cave. Ada left my side briefly, and I overheard her question the older of the two men.

'Have you ever lived in Southampton?'

'Why, yes, all my life. Still do,' he replied.

'Do you know if that old black cross is still outside the orphanage?'

'Yes, that's still there, but the building's long gone. It was closed after an abuse scandal twenty or thirty years ago and was then demolished. St Michael, it was. Saints and devils don't mix, that's for sure. The cross should have been a warning years before, what with the motto scratched into it by some well-meaning youngster. We all knew it when we were kids and used to walk on the other side of the street. "Be damned if you enter here." Scared the pants off of us, it did. Funny you should have mentioned that because the young woman's father was sent to that particular orphanage as a kid, poor sod. Life of torment if you ask me.'

Ada looked back at me. I could see that she had confirmed my worst thoughts and it was evident from her expression that I had definitely lost a lot more than what may have been seen as a passing fancy. She said nothing until after the two detectives had gone.

'Eddie, did you hear what was said about the cross and Marina's father, that he was killed in a hit and run? I'm certain he was your brother. What's more, there must be a connection. Two people from the same family don't get killed like that without a reason, which may put you right in the middle of it. We need to get some of Marina's DNA, if at all possible.

'Can you think of anything that might have been left in the cave that came in contact with her body? It's the only way we can prove your identity. If you can show that you are the next of kin to Marina, then it would be much easier to get you registered with social security and have a birth certificate in the name of Edward Dew.'

I thought hard about what she said. The question was, did I really want to be registered with anything? It was bad enough losing Marina. I know that sounds strange but that loss really did matter to me and then knowing that my twin brother had also been killed. The thing was, Ada was right. If ever I wanted to prove who I was, I really did need to have my name down somewhere. DNA would prove it and then at least I could get a copy of my birth certificate, maybe even a tax demand.

I searched my mind for anything that might have been missed, and then it clicked ... the mascara that Marina had been wearing. I had wiped her eyes with the tuft of rabbit fur which had been snagged on a thistle. It was wet with dew, and I just chucked it aside after I had wiped her face. There might be something on that, maybe in her tears. I just hoped it would be enough.

I didn't tell Ada at first. I had too many things to think about. It's stupid, I know, but I knew absolutely nothing about my twin, how he had lived or what he did for work. I knew nothing of him through all those years, and what's worse, as I got further away from setting down roots, my mind had drifted further off into another world, one in which relatives played no part. It was only Marina coming into my life that really jerked me out of it. Even then, bearing in mind that it had been a while since I'd found her, I still had trouble getting some things straight in my head. It would've been good to have something that I could have recognised or clued me in that I knew them.

I watched Ada as she flitted about the kitchen, cooking and tidying up. Every now and then, she'd look at me and ask, 'You alright there?' She was a comfort to be with. I hadn't thought about my presence being a burden when I arrived, but I could see in the way that she scratched through her purse for coppers that she couldn't really afford to have me staying there. Later that evening, I suggested to her that I should go. It was still warm at night and there was no frost, so I would've been alright.

'I won't hear of it. I need you here where I can keep an eye on you. Besides, I could do with your company and help around the farm. So no more of this nonsense.'

'Ada, look, it's not that I'm ungrateful, but I don't think you can afford to keep me. Your kindness to me could be your undoing. I really think I should leave.'

'No, you don't! You're not going anywhere, even if it means I have to tie you to a chair.' She laughed, came over to me and gave me a big hug. 'We'll be just fine. Let's take the bike to Castleton tomorrow, get a few provisions and draw some money out of the bank. I have a bit tucked aside for emergencies. We'll be alright for a while, don't you worry.'

***

I was up just before dawn and slipped away up onto the moor to look for the discarded rabbit fur. Ada told me to put a new envelope from one of the dresser drawers into my pocket to prevent any extra contamination. I don't understand much of this science stuff, but I did as she said. It didn't take me long to find it. The grass had been well trodden all around the site, but amazingly, the piece of fur, wet with dew again, was still untouched, caught up on a willow herb stem and glistening in the rays of the early morning sun. I used a thistle stem to lift it free, the black smudges of mascara still easily visible, and carefull folded it into the envelope and returned to the farmhouse.

Being on my own for so long had made me lose sight of some of the things that I should have done, one thing being to consider other people's feelings. Ada was so angry with me when I got back. 'Don't you ever do that again!' she shouted at me when I came in through the kitchen door.

'What?' I said, absolutely puzzled.

'You talked last night about leaving, and this morning, you disappeared without a word. I thought you'd left after all that we've gone through these past few days.'

I was stunned. It hadn't crossed my mind that she would be like that, you know, so worried about me. It touched me that she actually cared that much. 'I'm sorry, Ada. I didn't realise that you might have thought I'd gone. I went to get the DNA, and I thought I'd get it early so we wouldn't be too late to go to Castleton.'

She growled, releasing her anger and frustration. 'Remember, Eddie, we're in this together. You have to tell me what you're thinking so I'm not left out in the cold. We'll let it pass this time, but don't ever slip out again without saying a word.'

'But I thought you were still asleep.' I tried to excuse myself, but it didn't work.

'A little tap on the door or even a simple note on the dresser would've been the considerate thing to do.'

She handed me a mug of tea, and we sat in silence until, at last, she had calmed down. 'So, what's this DNA?'

'It's in the envelope. Rabbit fur with her tears and mascara on it. It might be useful if they can get some DNA from it.'

'Hopefully it might do the trick, but it's not guaranteed, though,' and with that, she popped the envelope into a small plastic container. 'I don't know how we'll get this checked out, but it'll be safe in here.' She dropped the box back into the dresser drawer, and in a more cheerful mood, we continued through breakfast until we were ready to leave.

'Ada, how are we going to carry the groceries?'

'Simple,' she said. 'In the cart.'

I imagined at that point that she meant a horse and cart, but no. Ada had a cart made from a painted wooden crate, two bicycle wheels, and an axle. She then bolted the whole contraption onto the rear of the tandem. Believe me, it worked. She certainly was

31

inventive though not terribly artistic. Looking around the barn, I could see quite an assortment of homemade accessories. It struck me that when she set her mind to do something, she never shied away from it, no matter how complicated or difficult the job may have seemed.

As it was, she had taken the helm, so to speak, and took on my troubles, for which I was grateful. I would have never known how to handle all of this had I been on my own as I've never considered myself to be a worldly person, and so much of this was above my head.

Chapter 5

It wasn't long after we left the farmhouse, pedalling at a steady pace with the box banging around behind us, that we saw Detective Constable Richards' car coming along the track towards the house.

'Goodness, I'm glad I haven't missed you. It's my day off and I thought I'd better keep you informed as to what's happening. Can we go back to the house? There are things I need to discuss, and I don't want anybody to know that I've been up here.'

We turned round and cycled back to the house following in the dust kicked up by Richards' car. Once there, we went indoors and Ada put the kettle on for tea.

'First of all, there are some things afoot which give me an uneasy feeling. No one seems to have made a connection between Marina Penrith and her father's death in Southampton. You would have thought someone would get curious about that, which makes me think that there's something going on. Sergeant Wragge's reputation for being bent has followed him, so I'm having him watched. Me being a local and he an outsider makes it a little bit easier. People up here don't like intruders too much.'

'So how does this involve us?' Ada interrupted.

'One of my mates saw Wragge in Eskdale talking to a couple of southerners who, he said, looked like trouble. My friend heard the name Dew mentioned. Now, I don't know whether he was referring to Marina, Marina's father, or you. My guess is that it was you. I mean, why should two men from down south, not policeman either, come all the way up here to talk about a road accident that happened in Southampton? It doesn't add up. So, you need to be on your guard. Having to work alongside Wragge makes me uncomfortable. Maybe it's for the best, though. At least I can keep my eye on him now.'

'Are you able to get some DNA checked out?' Ada asked as she went to the dresser drawer.

'Why do you ask? Whose DNA is it?'

I explained to Richards how I had gotten the sample. Ada suggested that there being three samples on the fur – Marina's, mine, and the rabbit's – it would be a good idea to take another sample from me.

'So, what's this about?' he asked.

Ada explained, 'Chances are that Edward is the twin brother of Marina's father and is, therefore, her uncle. He and his twin were taken to St Michael's orphanage after their parents were killed, and Eddie ran away from the place some years later. Ernest Dew, his brother, was sent off to Australia by the government and Edward never saw him again.'

'That's unbelievable and quite sad. I think I can get it analysed quite easily but not officially, you understand, and I'll ask for the results to be forwarded to you here and a copy sent off to me. Is that okay with you? It's possible that Wragge might have got wind of all this. I know he was talking to the detectives from Southampton for a good while when they were at the station. There's something going on, that's for sure.

'Look, it's going to take a few days to put this through, but I'll get the results back to you as soon as I can. In the meantime, keep out of sight, if that's at all possible, especially if you see or hear anything suspicious. I'd better be off now. Mind the road on that thing. I'll see you both soon. Oh, you'd better come out to the car, Edward. I've got a kit for a swab in the glove box.' He took a sample from inside my cheek, and then he was gone.

It was good to know that we had at least one ally. Ada had disappeared into her room and came down a few minutes later with a most unexpected item—a very large gun. This was no ordinary gun.

'My God, Ada! What on earth is that, an anti-tank gun?'

Ada chuckled as she swung the gun around the room. 'My husband George described it as an amalgam complete with homemade cartridges and a self-dispensing clip welded to the top. He used to take this out when there were poachers about. He'd fire it up into the trees and bring a branch or two down with it. Scared the poachers witless. They came up here twice but word got around, and I've not seen one anywhere near here since.

'You see, George was an engineer, a toolmaker to be more precise, and he made this in the barn from an old single-barrelled shotgun and some two-inch, cast-steel piping. He adapted the firing mechanism so that it would fire ten shots with this clip without having to reload and lined the barrel with copper. After that, he made up these special extra-long brass cases. He melted down some old brass ashtrays, then turned the cases up on his lathe, loading each with a lot of powder and three large ball bearings, the last of which was fixed firmly into the cartridge mouth. Anyway, I'll put this away for the moment, but I have a feeling that we might have need for it quite soon.'

I had never seen anything quite like it before. I dreaded to think what would happen if she fired it at anybody. I thought at the time it would take a strong person to survive the kick from firing that, but Ada seemed quite confident that she knew how to use it.

'It's getting late. It'll be lunchtime by the time we get to Castleton, so we'll have to have lunch there. What do you say to a glass of beer and some cheese and tomato sandwiches?'

'Sounds good to me, Ada.' I dared not tell her that I hadn't had a glass of beer for at least thirty years. That's what you must do if you want to keep out of sight. Either that or you can get so stuck on the stuff that you fall over on the road and get run over.

Truth be told, when we got back on the tandem to go home, it was as much as I could do to climb onto the saddle. 'One pint and Eddie's almost falling over,' my friends would say. It's a good thing that they weren't around. I would have never lived it down.

***

Everything was quiet for a couple of weeks. There was no more news regarding Marina or her murderers. I longed to visit the mortuary to see her again, but I knew that I had to put her away in a special part of my mind where I could see her alive in my imagination. Then Richards arrived one rainy morning. It was early October and the mornings were already becoming much darker.

'I have some news. Good or bad, that's for you to decide. Edward, Marina was your niece and Ernest was unquestionably your brother. It means that you are their next of kin, and I took the liberty of taking a look at the records of your brother's estate. It seems that everything he owned was to be passed on to Marina. Now that she is dead, you are the sole remaining member of the family. Have you got your birth certificate?'

'No, I haven't. When I ran away, I had nothing with me except the clothes on my back. Is that going to be a problem now that the DNA is conclusive?'

'I think so. To claim the estate, it will be necessary for you to prove your identity. I take it that you've never had a job or a social security number. Have you ever been to hospital or needed a doctor?'

'No. It's a healthy life living off the fruits of the wild.'

'Are you serious, Edward? You've never been ill?'

'Oh, I'm not saying that. I've had a couple of colds and a few infestations, but a sharp frost in winter usually gets rid of those. Do you know, the best thing to do when those little devils are most active is to take all your clothes off, roll about in the snow or heavy frost, then run about naked for half an hour, leaving your clothes spread out in the cold. When you get back, the lice and fleas are all gone.'

I saw Ada look at Richards with amusement. 'What?' I said, and she burst out laughing.

Richards sat down and spent several minutes just looking out of the window. I could tell that he wasn't seeing anything because his eyes were looking inwards as opposed to outwards. I'd seen this stare before when I spent time in a Sally hostel ten years ago. Some of the others were like me in their own ways, and we would share experiences of how we did things and so on. But if any of the staff were listening, they'd take on the same posture and empty look in their eyes. It was in the way they cocked their heads slightly and stood motionless looking out of the window, even when the curtains were closed.

Eventually, Richards asked, 'Edward, you haven't even asked what you might inherit from Marina and her dad. Don't you want to know?'

'I suppose so, but I don't really want anything. It's a shame that Marina never had any children. Mind you, if she had, they wouldn't have a mother now, and I know very well how that feels.'

'Edward, the fact remains that you are likely to inherit a large woodland, several farm buildings and four houses in Southampton. You're going to be quite a rich man!'

Richards looked excited as he gave me the news, but I found it really depressing. It seems odd to me, now that I've gotten used to it all, that at the time, I didn't want it. I would have willingly given everything to Ada. She would have known what to do with it better than me and it would have made her life all the sweeter ... or would it?

'Anyway, Edward, it does bring up a serious question: why are both your brother and niece dead? I'm puzzled that there has been no connection so far between the two deaths, which suggests either Special Branch involvement or something else that might be going on in the Hampshire constabulary. There is something decidedly fishy about it all.

'Go to Castleton. There is a solicitor there, John Hecket, whom I know quite well and can vouch for. Ada, go with Edward and take this report from the lab. It's quite conclusive. There's no doubt that there is a blood connection. He will probably be able to get a copy of the birth certificate sorted out as well.

'There is one other thing which is seriously bothering me. Nobody told me at the station that Wragge has gone on leave for two weeks. Bearing in mind that we are in the middle of an investigation into who killed Marina, I find it rather odd. I'm surprised he was allowed to go. I think there is something going on up here which is unusual, and I don't like it, not one bit. We normally have nothing to do with the southern police forces but I reckon that there is something from higher up that is putting some kind of pressure on the local police here.

'My advice to you is to lie low. It strikes me that there's something in your brother's and Marina's estate that someone is very keen to get their hands on. What I suggest is that you take this phone. If it rings, just answer it because it'll be me on the other end. If I hear of any danger, I'll call you.'

As he left, Ada looked at me with a bemused stare. 'What now, Eddie? I didn't expect all this when I found you in the barn. Come here, luv. We'll get through this and laugh about it after it's all done and dusted.'

Despite her hug, I could see that she was very troubled. We didn't say much during the rest of the day, but I watched her closely. It's strange, you know, having spent a lot of my life out in the wilds, avoiding any contact with humanity, that I suddenly found Ada was getting to me. It wasn't the kind of romantic love that people so often talk about, but more of a desire to no longer be on the outside.

It's true. I'd been in jail for vagrancy, which suited my purposes at the time. Ada's company and warmth was something else. She was getting inside me, a sort of dawning, you know, like belonging to a civilisation, good or bad. I never had to think about the effects of anything I did on someone else, but suddenly there was this sense of responsibility. I owed her that, just as she had given it to me.

I was beginning to wake up to the fact that I was part of a society, a human being, no longer a creature like a hedgehog or badger, fox or gull. I had started to think, to use my brain for things other than nuts and berries and the occasional treat of dog biscuits or beans. It was a very strange sensation. Ada had done all that for me.

Chapter 6

The weather was beginning to become unsettled. Warm winds from the southwest and cold winds from the northeast battled each other, and the inevitable torrents of rain fell to quench the thirsts of both. October had arrived with a vengeance. Dark night clouds swamped the moor with a cloak so black that hardly a chink of light could be seen from any direction.

It was several days after we had last seen Richards that a particularly rampant storm tore its way up from the south. The lightning that night was all around us as we sat on either side of the window with the lights out to watch the fury of the gods. Around eleven, another source of light could be seen, a steady moving light. Ada spotted it first.

'We've got company. I think we should go outside where we can't be found.' Immediately she grabbed her artillery in one hand and me in the other and pulled me through the door to the yard. 'Quick! Round the back where we can get a better look at them, but remember ... keep very, very quiet.'

The car slowly approached and stopped about fifty yards from the gate. With its lights out, it was hard to see who or what was coming. The lightning was perfect, though. As the storm continued, the flashes of light illuminated the whole area and we could see, momentarily, two figures cautiously approaching the house. Ada was poised with her gun raised, aiming into the branches of the trees that lined the edge of the track.

'Come on, my lovelies,' she whispered, 'just a little bit further.' There was a sudden clap of thunder just as Ada pulled the trigger. It took me quite by surprise. The recoil from the gun pushed her back with such force, and with me standing directly behind her, we both fell backwards. It was the first time that

I'd ever had a woman sitting on my lap, a not so unpleasant experience despite my having landed in a pool of very wet and sloppy mud.

'At least we've got some firewood for the winter,' she chuckled. I could see through the constant flashes of lightning that she had brought down a considerable quantity of small branches onto the track, just at the place where we had last seen the intruders.

'Damn it! They're getting away.' she whispered. 'Quick, grab my shoulders!' We could see the two men as if in a slowed-down silent film, parts of their movements blanked out between the ferocious flashes from the raging skies. 'Hold me!' she whispered, and raising the gun once again, she fired directly at the car as it was turning to make a retreat. For a few seconds, there was nothing. The car turned and drove away.

'Oh, bugger! I've never ever missed a shot before. I must be getting rusty.' But just as she uttered the last word, the car burst into flames. With a casual calmness in her voice, she said, 'Well, that was unexpected. It's going to be a bit of a problem, though. How am I going to explain this to the police, especially Richards? I'm not supposed to own a gun, not like this one, anyway. I don't think there will be much for us to see tonight, that's for certain. I don't reckon that it's right to try to save assassins either. Come on, Eddie. I think it's time to go indoors. Let the storm have its way.'

As we reached the door, there was an extremely large bang. The storm gods must have agreed among themselves and decided to help Ada out for as we turned to go through the door, a bolt of lightning struck the ground not two yards from the smouldering wreck. In all my years of living in the countryside away from the bright lights of the towns, I had never seen a thunderbolt strike so close before. The ground beneath our feet shuddered as it struck and then travelled sideways towards the hulk of the burned-out car. It seemed as if it was guided, devouring all in its path – the tyres, the hub caps, the bonnet, the boot – anything plastic, rubber or organic, meticulously, piece by piece, until nothing remained except the metal body, the chassis, and the engine block.

Of the two men in the car, there was nothing except charred bones and an assortment of teeth. Oh, and there were two belt buckles and two handguns, bullets all discharged. After knocking about in the wreck, the fireball rolled down the bank and into the river, where it finally quenched itself and disappeared.

I looked at Ada as we entered the dark house. 'I think we can turn the lights on now, can't we, Ada? That was a lucky break, wasn't it?'

'I'm not so sure of that, Eddie. It's almost like we're charmed. I can't make any sense of that, except ... Oh, Eddie, I just don't know where all of this is going, but we are in it right up to the hilt, you and me. After George, I didn't think I could want anyone around me, but now you're here and I want you to stay. Come here.'

We hugged for a long while. 'Ada,' I said quietly. 'I need to change my trousers and pants.' She gave me a really funny look. 'No,' I laughed, 'not that! I sat in the wet mud when you took that first shot.' At first, I thought that she believed I had wet myself, but by the look on her face, I think that she was thinking that it might have been something else.

'Thank goodness for that. We don't want all this to get too physical, do we?'

She was looking at me in a really odd way, and I had no idea what she was referring to.

***

The following morning, the mobile telephone that Richards had given to Ada began to ring. We both looked at it with dread. 'What do we do?' I asked her.

'Answer it, I suppose. What did he say? Press this button, or was it that one?' The phone continued to ring.

'Bugger the damn thing! Be quiet, will you?' She pressed a button but said nothing.

'Hello, Ada, are you there?' The voice was a hoarse whisper, as if the caller was uncertain as to who might be listening.

'Yes, I'm here,' she whispered back.

'It's Richards here. Are you both safe? I got some news late last night that a couple of men were asking details about the roads around your area. I couldn't get away to warn you. Is everything alright?'

'Nothing that the storm couldn't deal with. I think you need to come over. There was a thunder bolt last night and a car was destroyed up the lane.'

'I'll be up later this morning, about eleven. See you then.'

'Now that's a funny thing. I must be going paranoid because I'm not sure if that was Richards or someone impersonating him. We'll have to wait and see. He whispered everything as if somebody was listening. I have an uneasy feeling, Eddie. He said he'll be here around eleven, so we'll see who turns up.

Richards did arrive more or less on time. I met him up by the wreck of the car while Ada sat on a high bank overlooking the track, keeping herself out of sight. Her rifle was cocked and ready to shoot at any sign of trouble. She had told me, 'If there's any funny business, just run. I'll deal with it from up here.'

Richards looked very agitated. He looked at the car wreck almost as if he couldn't believe what he saw. He spotted two pistols and bent down to pick one up. It was still too hot to handle and he dropped it immediately.

'Where's Ada? '

'Oh, she'll be along in a few minutes,' I replied. 'I think she's out looking for mushrooms.'

Richards said nothing but scratched around in the debris looking for anything that might identify the two raiders. 'Whose land is this?' he asked in an aggressive tone.

'Why?' I asked.

'If it's Ada's, she'll have to pay for the wreck to be taken away.'

Ada arrived, without her gun, I hasten to add, just in time to hear the last few words. 'It'll have to stay there then, won't it. It's not on my land anyway. That bit belongs to the National Trust, I think. All I know is that my property is up to my gate, but after that...'

'How did you do this? I could arrest you for murder, you know!' Richards was kicking the toe of his shoe into the ashes, obviously trying to stay in control.

'No, you couldn't. There's absolutely no evidence of foul play on our behalf. Any fool could see that the car was struck by a thunderbolt, and looking at those two guns, I'd say that we are lucky to be alive. So, we're going to my sister's place in Whitby until all this is sorted out. I think you had better go now if you don't mind. We have some packing to do. By the way, here's your telephone.'

'Give me your sister's address before you leave in case I need to contact you. Forensics will be here in a day or two to sort this mess out.' He hurriedly scribbled down the address that Ada recited, and with that, he turned on his heel and departed.

'Just as I thought. He's caught up in it, probably as deeply as Wragge but coming in from a different angle, and I think he is way out of his depth. I wonder who's pressuring him. Eddie, it seems to me that there are two sides to this business, and neither of them mean us any good. George always said, "Never trust a copper if it's bent. It'll never go in the meter." By the way, my sister in Whitby won't be able to welcome us. She's in the cemetery, in the kiddies' section there. She died from scarlet fever the year before I was born.'

I was a bit shocked. 'I'm sorry about that, Ada. But what have you got in mind?'

'George's secret bunker. You know where I was hiding just now? Well George had a notion that we should always have a hiding place ready in case the world went topsy turvy. As luck would have it, there's a good-sized cave up there which he used to play in when he was a kid. So he adapted it for the two of us. It's got a bed, cupboards, and fresh water from a spring that runs from the back. There's even a portable chemical loo up there. What's more, there's a small wood burner for cooking and keeping the temperature up in winter, but we'll only be able to use that after dark when the smoke won't be seen. We used to go up there quite a lot in the summer. It was always nice and cool up there.'

I couldn't help thinking that Ada was a bit peculiar, an adventure seeker. My instinct would have been to take to my heels and run off across the moor to somewhere even more secluded. But she was right. We needed to see this one through, right up to the bitter end. I owed it to both Marina and my brother.

George had certainly been very clever. He had even devised a listening post to detect any intruders that might be in the vicinity of the cave or the house. In the alcove of the spring at the back of the cave, he had made use of a very lightweight wheel-driven kind of dynamo which, using the flowing water, was able to generate just enough power to transmit a voice picked up through an old oil drum. This was open at one end and contained the diaphragm of an ancient wireless speaker linked to another of the same type within the cave. The drum was half hidden a short distance away down the bank and linked up with a wire running through a copper pipe. I didn't know how it really worked but it reminded me of the two-bean-can system which some of the kids played with down at the orphanage when I was a youngster.

A day later, we moved in. It was surprisingly comfortable and we ate well, but bedtime came as a bit of a shock.

'I'm going to get washed now.' Ada had heated some water on the stove and commenced to undress. I had kept my eyes down not wanting to embarrass her by staring, but suddenly there she was, completely naked. I didn't know quite where to put myself, and I quickly turned away again. It was as if she didn't know I was there. When she had finished and emptied the basin, she put her nightgown on and got into bed.

'Your turn! There's some more hot water in the other pan.'

And so, I followed suit, doing my best to hide all the things that I thought I shouldn't show. I looked at the bed and then around the cave. There was no alternative. I squeezed in beside her and stayed as still as I possibly could. I hardly dared to breathe, but then I felt her hand on mine. 'Goodnight, Eddie. Sleep well.' She turned over and before long, both of us were fast asleep.

***

The following morning, Ada woke me with a cup of tea kept hot in a thermos overnight. By 8.30 am, we were back in the house where we ate breakfast. It was around 9:30 am when I heard the rumbling of a van coming along the track. We locked the doors and slipped out the back of the house and up into the cave. Ada freed the dynamo, and within a few minutes, we could faintly hear the voices from down below. There was a lot of clattering, stuff being moved around, the clicking of a camera, and then a voice came through, loud and clear.

'Why did Richards think these two were Special Branch? I don't think so, not with those two pistols and bloody silencers, too. They're definitely not police issue 9 mm Berettas by the look of them, more like the sort of things hired killers use. What were they doing up here? And what's Richards up to? Better check the house, see if anyone is in there. They may or may not have been able to escape. I just hope they did.'

After that, we heard them muttering as they continued picking over the bones and teeth and other debris. 'Nothing much to go on in this lot. I wonder what these ball bearings were for, though? I suppose they might have been for some kind of catapult, but it's just a guess. There's no sign of anything like that lying around that I can see.'

After another hour, we heard the rumble of the van departing. When all was silent, we slipped down, back to the house. The door had been forced open.

'Bugger!' muttered Ada. 'More bloody repairs.'

'Ada, do you often swear?'

'Yes, quite often. Cats do it, so why shouldn't I?'

I laughed. I always thought that women didn't use language like that. Well, that was what I had been told. Fortunately, the lock plate was the only thing that had come away and a few longer screws would secure it, at least for the time being.

'I'll fix it,' I offered.

'No, we'll leave it just as it is. Otherwise, they'll know that we've been back. I'll do it myself later. For now, you can get a carton from the barn so we can collect the rest of the provisions. I think washing will be easier done in here, provided one of us keeps watch. At least we can stay clean.'

When she said, 'Keep watch', I couldn't stop myself from giggling, which did not go unnoticed.

'In the days ahead, Eddie, you will see a lot more of me than you bargained for, and it won't just be me washing myself in your company either. Don't forget, there are people out there who want you and probably me dead. So, when I say keep watch I really mean it, and furthermore, if you want to see me get undressed, don't be shy. I might even invite you to scratch my back.'

Was that an invitation or a soft rebuke, I thought to myself. But she was right. There were people out there, and keeping an eye constantly open was imperative for us to stay alive. There was no dithering. She always seemed so self-confident, always one step ahead of the game and two steps ahead of me. It was an odd sensation, being hunted down but also feeling safe with her.

***

We spent two days and nights up in the cave without any sign of intruders. But on the third day around 3.00 am, we heard on the speaker the sound of two vehicles approaching. I awoke first and alerted Ada.

'That's Richards' voice, isn't it?' I whispered.

'Yes, but keep quiet. I hope they don't start smashing the house up too much. Stay here with the rifle, and if they come out before I'm back, shoot up into that tree there. With luck, that will get them back into the house and give me a chance to get back up here.'

'Ada, what are you planning on doing?'

'Nick a car,' she said with a quiet giggle.

'Are you serious, Ada? You could get hurt out there!'

'Stop worrying, Eddie! I'll be right back,' she said, putting on her raincoat and boots. She quietly slipped out and disappeared.

There was a clear sky and a half-moon, which allowed me to see the door to the house quite easily. I could hear a drawn-out hissing sound, not very loud. Before long, Ada was back at my side.

'Any movement yet?' she whispered.

'No, nothing outside, but they're making a bit of a racket in the house.'

'Bastards! That Richards is going to pay for this.' I believed her.

Eventually the search came to an end and the four men returned to their cars. The engines started, but as the second vehicle turned to go back up the lane, it stopped.

'Richards!' the voice shouted. 'I've got a bloody puncture and the spare's as flat as a pancake. I'll never get this back along that track tonight. We'll have to come with you, and you can drop us off on the way.' This was followed by more cursing, and finally, Richards' car lights disappeared into the distance.

'What did you do down there, Ada?'

'I let the air out of one front tyre and put a hole in the spare. There's a foot pump in the barn, so we now have a set of wheels.'

'But you haven't got any keys for it so you won't be able to start it.'

'Seriously, Eddie, you worry too much! You know, George had a thing about survival. That's why he fitted out the cave. He taught me all sorts of things, from first aid to martial arts and how to hotwire a car. It was all good fun, though. The car whose tyre I flattened looks like an old Ford and will be dead easy to start. But we had better move quickly before anybody returns to collect the car.' She fetched me the pump, and within an hour, we were on the road heading south towards York.

Fortunately, there was plenty of fuel in the car. As dawn broke, we pulled into a café car park to have some breakfast. Ada had just enough cash to cover the bill, and soon, we were back on the road. It was a long time since I went anywhere by car and my stomach wasn't quite sure whether it was happy or not. It might have been the rushed breakfast, something that I was not quite used to. Mind you, everything considered, sitting in a car certainly beat walking or peddling the tandem, that was for sure.

Chapter 7

'Where are we going, Ada?'

'To George's nephew, Dick. He's a lawyer in York. But first, we'll find the police station and park the car outside. Then we'll walk to Dick's office in the town centre and tell him what's been going on. I'm sure he'll know what to do. We might have to stay there for a few days because we need to get your birth certificate sorted out. I've got Richards' printout in my bag, so we can give that to Dick and he can do some legal work on what your brother and Marina have left behind. He'll find out whose dealing with it in Southampton. Then off we go to the seaside. That's something to look forward to, isn't it?'

Ada was so bright and breezy about it all that one wouldn't think we'd been up since three that morning. She glanced round at me and said, 'When this is sorted out, Eddie, I'll show you how to fight and maybe a few other things.'

I wasn't quite sure what she meant by that, so I put it to the back of my mind for the while and concentrated on trying to stay awake.

❀

It was still quite early when we reached York, where we abandoned the car outside the police station, parked on double yellow lines.

'That'll get it noticed soon enough.' Ada laughed as she half-dragged me across the road and down a side street. She seemed to know her way around the city, and before I knew it, we were standing outside the office of Brignall & Sprain Associates.

'Right, here we are, bit early, though. I need to draw out some cash, and then we'll have some coffee and a bun. What do you think?'

By 10 am, we were back at the office just in time to see Dick Robely unlock the main door.

'Hello, Ada! Come in. How are you? Still up there on the moor? And you are...?' he said looking in my direction.

'Dick, this is my dear friend and new housemate, Edward Dew. He's the one in need of your assistance.'

The formalities were brief, and in short order, Ada had explained all that had happened. Dick was tied up for the rest of the morning but asked us to return around 4 pm to discuss our options and who to contact. We returned at the requested hour.

'I've had a word with an old colleague who retired to the Isle of Wight, and from what he tells me, there's a rumour going around in Southampton over a strange land grab. Apparently, there's a great deal of money resting on the outcome for certain unnamed individuals, including someone from overseas.

'I also contacted the registrar to check whether a DNA declaration would be acceptable to enable your friend to receive a duplicate birth certificate. He said that it is not a regular means but it's possible, and he's checking on it. He expects to call me back tomorrow. I didn't give him your details, however, as we obviously don't know who to trust at the moment, least of all Hecket at Castleton. There are rumours that he is more corrupt than the contents of a waste pipe.

In addition to that, there has been a spate of deaths in Southampton without any obvious crimes having been committed because they've all been registered as accidental. So, I'm not even sure whether the local coroner can be trusted either.

'What is really sinister about all of this is that one would expect the newspapers to be full of details about your niece, Eddie, bearing in mind that there has been a search for her for at least six weeks. But there's not a word about her body being found. The police or someone in the government has put a gag order on news of her death.

'You're actually in a great deal of danger, that's for sure. In fact, if it is known that you are here in York, I think we might all be in for a spot of trouble. My advice to you is to keep your heads down. As far as the car is concerned, I have somebody I can trust at the police station, and I will give him a call to see who comes to claim it, that's if anybody dares.'

'Dick, you have been so helpful, but one other thing that we need to do is to find accommodations for a while. I've got a little bit of money that I've been saving, but if you know of a cheap hotel, we would be grateful.'

'Ada, dear Ada. My sister, Ruth, has a bungalow on the outskirts of town. She said that if ever I needed it for a client, a respectable client that is, then I should feel free to use it. You two look respectable to me.' Dick laughed. 'Be her guest. I'm sure she will accommodate you. After all, you're like family. One thing, though ... no partying, Eddie! You look as if you can get a bit wild at times, doesn't he, Ada?'

I put it down to the way Ada had cut my hair, but his slap on my back nearly knocked me over. I'm sure it was all well meant. Dick called a taxi for all of us to go to his sister's bungalow. As the taxi waited, Dick bid us farewell and was about to return to his office when he turned back. 'Look, you two, you're here on holiday. Use the names Mr and Mrs Grantham should anybody ask and when you telephone me. Here's my number. Meet me at the Amicus Club at midday tomorrow and we'll have some lunch together. It's just around the corner on Hampton Street. Here, I'll jot down the address for you.'

***

The bungalow was more than comfortable. Neither Ada nor I had ever known how to luxuriate, but now it seemed like we were about to. There was hot water in abundance, a shower cubicle for two, and a bath. In the kitchen, there was tea and coffee, proper coffee, not from a jar. In the freezer, there were vegetables and soups in little bags. Not fifty yards away on the corner of the street was a baker's and also a greengrocer's shop. Beside the bungalow was a garage with two bikes, and next door was a beautiful grey and white cat. I could have lived there forever.

The following day, we met Dick for lunch at his club. The restaurant was quite fancy and I wished we had had nicer clothes to wear. I felt a bit out of place but Ada didn't seem too bothered so I guessed we looked okay.

Seated next to Dick was a thirty-something gentleman wearing a smart suit and tie and spit-shined shoes. Both Dick and the gentleman rose as we approached the table.

'Ada, Eddie, I'd like you to meet Thomas Swain.' We politely shook hands and everyone took a seat. I couldn't help but notice Thomas's unusual cuff bracelet. On the front part was an emblem of a viper with shiny blue opals for eyes. It was set on a wide, shiny metal cuff. I wondered if it symbolised anything. It looked quite expensive, but as I've never owned a piece of jewellery in my life, it was hard to tell. It led me to believe that Mr Swain must have been making good money in his position.

Dick continued, 'Tom worked with Joseph and I some years ago as a junior on a complicated legal case which we ultimately won, thanks in great part to his research capabilities.'

Tom seemed to visibly blush. 'Don't pay any attention to him. I've paid him handsomely to say nice things about me in case there are important people within earshot.' We all laughed so hard, the table shook. It definitely broke the ice. Thomas wasn't as stuffy as he looked.

'Ada and Eddie, I hope you don't mind but I've taken the liberty of ordering a nice meal for each of you as I have a meeting in forty-five minutes. You both can stay as long as you like.'

'Thank you, Dick. That's very kind of you,' said Ada.

I'd never been to a classy restaurant like that except for the odd fast-food takeaway places where I was sure to find some freshly discarded morsels at a certain time of day. Being unfamiliar with the formalities, I decided to follow what everyone else did.

Speaking directly to Ada and me, Dick answered the question we both probably had on our minds. In a low tone, he explained, 'I asked Tom to join us today because he is now an adviser to the government's environmental affairs office and has kindly agreed to help us with the land and property you now own.

'As there now seems to be too many hands in the pot, I have asked Tom to find out exactly who is vying for the land and why. Of course, this is all off the record and must be kept confidential. Tom's identity must never be discussed with anyone except between us. In repayment for this considerable and risky undertaking, I have offered Tom my firstborn...' We all broke out in laughter, and Ada spit out her sip of wine. 'But since that would be a miraculous phenomenon and largely unlikely, we have agreed on a quid pro quo arrangement. Haven't we, Tom?'

Everyone was laughing hysterically, so it must have been funny, but he lost me at firstborn. I was sure Ada would explain it to me later.

Not to be outdone, Tom said, 'Since I can't have your firstborn, be assured this is going to cost you dearly, Dick.' More snickering followed.

Ada said, 'In all seriousness, we are extremely grateful for your support, both of you. We had been quite lost as to how to proceed, but you seem to have everything in hand, I think. Obviously, we'd be happy to provide you with any information or assistance you may need.'

At that point, two waiters approached our table with our meals and we quickly changed the subject.

Shortly after we had finished our meals, Tom rose and said, 'Please excuse me. I need to meet with my friend over at the bar. I believe he has a bridge he wants to sell me. Ada, Eddie it was a pleasure meeting you. I'm sure we'll be seeing each other again soon.'

Dick called out to him, 'Tom, give me a call at the office tomorrow before noon, will you?'

'I will,' he said and sauntered over to the bar where a well-dressed, middle-aged man was waiting.

No sooner had Tom left the table, Dick beckoned a thin young man over to join us. I had seen him watching us for some time and had a slightly uneasy feeling about him. Almost in a whisper, Dick said, 'This is a second party I want you to meet who can provide us with information we might need.

'Ada, Eddie, I would like you to meet Oscar Rinton. He has been working within an environmental protection group which, though they have no political approval, keep other environmental groups informed of what is going on in the backrooms of the government and certain other agencies. Oscar, meet Ada and her close friend and admirer, Edward Dew.' Dick followed that introduction with a wink directed at me.

When he said 'admirer', I could feel the blood rush to my cheeks. Clearly embarrassed, I side-glanced at Ada, who was looking straight at me with a slight smile.

'It's okay, Eddie, I think Ada feels the same way about you.'

That made it worse. I knew I had nothing real to offer Ada except companionship. Deep down, though, I knew there was something else, but it was something that I didn't quite know how to cope with. When you've spent your life as I have, it's sometimes very difficult to understand what people mean to each other. I'm good with cats. I know them. But people, Ada ... they're so complicated.

Oscar obviously knew his business well. He explained he had contacts from all over Britain and Europe who were watching for any moves that the oil and mineral extraction companies were making and that, he added, was where Marina and Ernest's problems arose. They were the proprietors of a certain patch of land, Ernest's inherited farm a little way in from the coast and a few miles to the east of Southampton.

'This is what I know so far in your case, Eddie. Is it okay for me to call you Eddie?'

'Of course.'

Ada edged in a bit closer. I was glad because my confidence in understanding what was going on was lacking, especially under the stress. Looking back at it now, I think it's crazy that I was so, what would one say, self-conscious in the personality department.

'Well, as I understand it, your brother's foster father in Australia left your brother, Ernest, a large plot, around 400 hectares, which straddled the old south track along the coast towards Portsmouth. Most of it is gone now, dropped into the sea, the track, that is. Now, there are two lots involved in trying to grab that land, and neither of them is very nice, which may explain why Ernest was knocked off and then Marina taken and murdered. They don't care what they do nor how they do it, you know, and if they have got wind of you, which I think they have, your newfound life will be very short, and that goes for Ada as well. So, I'm telling you to watch out and don't trust anyone, present company excluded, of course.

'Right, now for the worst bit. There is a Russian agency and a government Secretary involved in this, but more of that later. What you need to do now, Eddie, is to stake your claim as soon as possible. Otherwise, the land will be snatched right from under you by someone working within the local planning office. The property would be handed over to either a particularly nasty group from Russia or to an equally distasteful Anglo-American petrochemical group. I'm not sure which has the upper hand. You must excuse me, but under the circumstances, I daren't name any names. There's an old saying that applies here: "The walls have ears".'

'Now, I've heard the Russian party is linked to the government environment Secretary. Working for him is a local county councillor who stands to lose a huge bonus if he can't swing the deal to acquire your land for them. And why do they all want your land, you may ask? Simple. There must be some kind of rich mineral deposits there. Looking at the number of people who have disappeared recently in the area of metallurgy, one can only assume that there is a lot of money at stake in such a deal, that's if they can push it through. It's amazing how little life is worth when these greedy pigs are at the trough.'

It was at that point that Dick rose. 'I need to go back to my office now. I have an appointment at three. Ada, Eddie, I'll see you this evening about seven o'clock at the bungalow. I'd really like to have a chat with you about old times and what George was up to.' Then turning to Oscar, 'Keep in touch, Oscar. Any information, I'm sure will be of great help. Bye for now, everyone,' and Dick was gone.

Oscar looked nervous. 'Look here, you two. Everything I say to you must never go any further. I've got loads of other stuff on the go, and though I would love to be with you right to the very end on this, I don't think it's going to be possible. The thing is that you don't want to be seen with me because if they are watching you, then they will see me and that is definitely something that I don't want. Those bastards are completely ruthless. Look, you'll be here for a couple of weeks, I suppose. If I call, I will give the name Joplin and I'll use a Scottish accent. If the accent is wrong, then you will know the caller is not me and that I've been grabbed. Okay, good luck! Hope to see you soon.'

Ada and I watched him go. Neither of us had noticed at first that he had a slight limp and that his left shoulder was drooping considerably below the right one.

'I have a feeling he's been in a lot of trouble in the past and I hate to say it,' Ada whispered, 'but I think he's got a lot of enemies. There are people in the government who probably have him in their sights, and he will be marked down as a terrorist just so they can lock him away. I hope not, but one can never be too sure these days. We'd better go now before we get noticed.'

I was beginning to think this whole thing was way over my head, what with all the secrecy and uneasiness. But Ada seemed so confident, I was sure it would all fall into place.

Chapter 8

The Secretary of State for the Environment was about to leave his office when his private phone rang. 'Yes?'

'Basilisk here. Can you talk?'

'What's your port of entry?' the Secretary asked.

'SCT 5,' he responded.

'You've got one minute.'

'Target Oscar has been colluding with the land heir and his girlfriend at a meeting set up by their solicitor friend. I suspect the target has informed them of the Russian involvement but I'm not sure how much they know.'

The Secretary slammed his fist on his desk. 'Dammit!' Those lunatic environmental anarchists have taken it too far now. After a short pause, 'I need you to infiltrate. Can you do that?'

'I think I can. But I'll need an asset from MI6 to provide background information. Have you got anyone?'

The Secretary thought for a second. 'I have someone in the Records and Microfilm Department. I'll have her call you. Her codename will be Anemone. Get back to me as soon as you hear anything. Stay clean, and for God's sakes, don't get burned!'

Digging into his inside jacket pocket, the Secretary brought out what appeared to be a slim calculator. Using a stylus, he pressed several numbers and held the object to his ear.

'Dexter,' said the voice on the other end.

'It's Skorpius. I've got a job for you. I need you to engage and eliminate a loose cannon.'

Chapter 9

Very little happened over the following days, except Ada and I got to know a little more about each other. We met with Dick regularly, but progress was slow as we waited for news from Dick's contact on the Isle of Wight. I finally received my proof of identity through the good services of the Southampton registrar who, as luck would have it, was standing in as a holiday relief officer. Dick had known the man since his school days and doubted that he would be aware of any corruption in any of his appointments throughout the country. It was a chance that Dick thought was worth taking as any ties to the registration application would be lost in all the other stuff that passes through the offices of a city as large as Southampton.

From that point on, we were all faced with some terrifying options. Ada explained, 'The problem for Dick, as involved as he is with us, is whether or not to represent you in your claim of the estate. By doing so he could alert the other parties as to our whereabouts. It would be better for us to leave the area and be out of the way should there be any follow up. Dick thinks that it will be unlikely that his family connection to me will be discovered straightaway and that representing you in the claim would not place him at any great risk. I just hope that he's right.'

Dick opened a bank account in his name and placed enough funds for us to live on for several months. He gave his account's debit card to Ada.

He also provided a copy of the documents relating to my claim to Tom Swain should his own office be raided. It all seemed so cloak and dagger but as he said, 'These are dangerous people that we are dealing with. They have a history of bloodletting, and I just hope that none of mine or yours flows down the same drain.'

Ada suggested that we should make our way to Portsmouth. Dick agreed that it was for the best and brought out his youthful aspiration, as he put it, his old Triumph 500 motor bike, complete with sidecar.

'Ada, I know you can ride one of these. I've heard the stories about you and George, but remember, don't go over the speed limit unless you really need to, and try not to attract too much attention. I think you'll be seen as just another pair of old codgers on an old bike, probably the best cover that I can offer you. Remember to use the name Grantham when you call and I'll open a spurious file under that name with just junk about litigation for dog fouling. That will keep the hounds off the scent.' I could see by the twitch at the corner of his mouth that he was laughing to himself.

With the prospect of being on the road again, I took the opportunity to bid a last farewell to the luxurious bathroom in the bungalow. Ada was busy studying the Michelin road map for the journey ahead, so I ran myself a hot bath and decided to wallow for half an hour or so. It was a great excuse to do some thinking and rid myself of tiny areas of grime that hot water had not yet discovered.

As so often happens in the WC, one's mind turns over the previous days' events, and the turmoil that presented itself to me drove me to think. Eventually, it was the DNA on which I became most focused. Why was it so important? I had almost forgotten.

When I found Marina, it was probably the last thing in the world that I would have thought of. My relationship with her was obviously one of need. I didn't realise how desperately I needed company until I found her. I seriously wanted her to be alive. But the silly thing was that if she was not dead, let's imagine, then if she awoke and saw me, she would have been terrified. So the fact remains that for me to have had any kind of relationship with her, she actually needed to be dead. It's a horrible thought, I know, but how else can it be explained? I even talked to her, imagined her replies, told her stories about the animals on the moor and about the fish in the river. It fulfilled something inside me, call it what you will.

Suddenly, along comes the family connection, the DNA, and with it, an entirely different set of rules. Not only had I lost my love for Marina to the mortuary, but I had also lost a large part of my family. I had been cheated out of knowing my nearest and, may I use the expression, dearest, and a kind of anger set in.

The truth of the matter was that Ada fulfilled my need for company and became a substitute for Marina in the days that followed. Things have changed now, and Ada and I are much more complete. She actually got me to start thinking about, you know, being real. And that's the beauty about a long soak in a warm bath. It helps one to think, file a history in the right order and measure its worth.

The days were shortening and the chill of winter was already spreading its fingers into the night air. Travelling on a motor bike was not the best option at that time of year unless one could stay warm and dry enough to battle against the elements. So, using Dick's debit card, we bought enough warm underwear and motorcycle gear for the trek down south. Before long, we were on the road to Portsmouth. Dick had given us the contact number for his friend on the Isle of Wight, who was now fully acquainted with what was going on. His name was Joseph Puttick.

Once we reached Northampton, the weather somewhat improved. There was no more of the light drizzle that fogged up Ada's goggles, and the road was less slippery.

We stayed overnight in a motel, had a good breakfast which included mushrooms, always a favourite of mine. But they were a little disappointing, not so fresh, and cooked in oil instead of butter. That was something that I had learned years ago at a hostel in Bristol. The cook there told me that they have to be cooked that way, slowly in a frying pan with butter and maybe a little pepper and a few grains of salt. Sorry, I'm rambling again.

From there we stopped off in Guildford for lunch before taking a detour to Winchester. There, we stayed overnight to work out our next move. We decided to contact Oscar first to see if he had anything new to tell us. He was quite excited that we had travelled so far but said that he was in Cornwall. He asked Ada to call him the following evening so that we could arrange to meet up.

In the meantime, we drove down to Portsmouth and booked in at a bed & breakfast in South Hayling Island, about as quiet a place that one could find in November. So far so good. Our tracks were well covered with little chance of being spotted in that area.

Ada called Oscar as arranged. He sounded a little nervous and soon dropped the Scots accent.

'What's up? Is there some trouble, Oscar?' I heard Ada ask.

'Yes, I got a message this morning from a friend who told me that my cover has been blown. We've had a spy in our camp, and several of the group have been caught up by a division working from within the police, which seems to be directly controlled by someone in Whitehall. I can't think of who they or the spy might be. The worst of it is that we don't expect to see any of our friends again. This has happened before and they never come back, so for the time being, we've had to disband and disperse. I think that this phone is okay, but I'm going to chuck it anyway just in case. Look, I'll see you at Tesco's in Havant tomorrow morning around ten. I'll be watching out for you.'

I had been listening close to Ada's hand as she held the phone. I could feel her warmth on my cheek as she pressed the phone to her ear. Oscar had gone, and I had forgotten to remove my face. Suddenly, I was aware that she was stroking my cheek with her thumb, her hand covering my ear. She turned and softly kissed my forehead. She was looking straight into my eyes.

'Come on, you,' she said, breaking the spell. 'Buck up, now. It's supper time!' There's nothing like a touch of raw reality to spoil a dream.

***

When we arrived at Tesco's car park the next morning, we noticed that an area had been cordoned off by the police. Ada approached one of the trolley collectors at the trolley bay.

'What's going on over there?'

'Oh, some druggie took an overdose and died stuffed into one of these trolleys,' came the somewhat disinterested reply. It was almost as if it was an everyday occurrence.

'How did he get into the trolley if he overdosed?' Ada queried.

'Well, someone must have put him in there, mustn't they!' came the slightly aggressive response.

'Did you see him?'

'Yeah, it was me who found him, wasn't it!'

'What did he look like?'

'Dead, of course! Sorry, lady, but I've got to get on with my work.'

'Thanks anyway, mate.'

Ada grabbed my hand and we rushed over to where the crowd was standing behind a barricade of yellow police tape. We walked around the perimeter, looking for an opening to get a view of the scene.

He was sitting in the trolley, legs drawn up to his chin, his head leaning back against the handlebar. It was Oscar.

Ada gasped. 'We need to get out of here!' she muttered and dragged me by the hand back to the car. I followed her lead in shock.

Ada made a detour as we left Havant back toward Hayland Island, taking a lot of country lanes to ensure that we weren't followed. We rode out speechless, both of us numb with disbelief. Ada broke the silence. 'Who could have done this to him? Why?' After a pause, 'Oh, my goodness! Maybe he was followed. But how did they know we were meeting here?'

I had no answers for her. I looked out the window as we passed naked trees and dry, thirsty hedgerows lining the roadway. Between their lower branches, I could see snuff-coloured fields and rolling hills. It reminded me of my safe haven in the moors and how content I was, away from the evils of humanity, before all this happened.

That night, Ada hugged me close to her. It was the first time that I can ever remember feeling so much comfort in my whole life. We were becoming what we were pretending to be: a middle-aged devoted couple. At least I think that was how we were seen. We sat there, on the edge of the bed, looking at our feet. You know, Ada has very nice feet, not like mine. Mine are quite grim to look at ... over-used, one might say. It didn't help having a hole in my sock either.

'You know, Ada, this is beginning to feel just like it was when I ran away from St Michael. Never sure which way to go, frightened that I might have been seen then caught and taken back to the orphanage. The only difference now is that we're both in this together, and it's not a matter of being caught but more a case of avoiding being killed. What sort of people are these that can go about murdering people?'

'Evil people, Eddie, the worst sort. All they worship is money, nothing else. I'm going to ring Dick tomorrow. He might have some ideas about what we should do next. I wonder about his contact on the Isle of Wight. He seems to know quite a lot about what's going on.'

Chapter 10

He picked up the phone on the first ring. 'Basilisk.'

A sultry female voice responded. 'It's Anemone. I understand you require assistance.'

'Who sent you?'

'Let's not play games, Basilisk. I don't have the time. The Secretary gets impatient, and so do I.'

'You must know him well,' he said, attempting to get further confirmation of her ties. She did not respond. Basilisk continued, 'I'm working with the Secretary on gathering intelligence on...'

Anemone interrupted, 'The Secretary has briefed me on your project. What do you need from me?'

What an intriguing woman, he thought. Under different circumstances, he would have presumed that she was making an offer he wouldn't refuse. He also noted a slight eastern European accent though that was not too concerning since he was aware that MI6 hired foreign-born British citizens. 'I need some background information on the heir to the Southampton lands and property, including his girlfriend. Names are Edward, also known as Eddie, Dew and Ada Gampe.' He spelled both surnames for her.

'Have you a date of birth or any other information that could assist me in my search?'

'All I've gathered from newspaper clippings is that the properties were inherited from Edward's deceased brother, Ernest Dew, and Ernest's daughter, Marina Penrith of Portsmouth, also deceased.'

'I'll start the process through OSINT and see what I can get. I'll get back to you within forty-eight hours,' she said.

'I'd like to treat you to dinner in appreciation of your service, Anemone.'

'Sorry, Basilisk. I don't mix business with pleasure,' and she hung up.

Chapter 11

Ada telephoned Dick in his office in the early morning hours and let me listen in on the conversation. 'Hello, could I speak to Mr Robely, please? It's Mrs Grantham.'

I remember that Ada tried to be as calm as possible, but I could still hear a slight anxiety in her voice.

'Mrs Grantham, Mr Robely mentioned that you might call and gave me permission to tell you. Last night, he was taken into police custody. I'm afraid I have no further details, but before he was apprehended, he left a note for you regarding the litigation in which you are involved. Are you in a position to collect the note from here at the office?'

'No,' Ada replied slowly. 'I'm on holiday in Edinburgh at present.' There was a pause. I could see that Ada was weighing the situation up, and then she added, 'Is it possible for you to read to me the contents so I'll know if I should return earlier?'

'Certainly. It reads as follows: "Dear Mrs Grantham, about the litigation regarding dog fouling. There was a similar case to yours two years ago which was handled by my friend and colleague Joseph Puttick, now retired. I have spoken to him about your case and am pleased to inform you that he is willing to give you all the relevant details and representation to deal with the claim against you. You can telephone him at the following number for an appointment".'

Ada jotted down the phone number and thanked the secretary for her help. Turning towards me, she said, 'What in the world is going on! I hope Dick is alright. I can't imagine how they've managed to haul him in. Do you suppose we were spotted together with poor Oscar? I think this is getting really horrible. I would have never believed that there's so much underhanded business going on in the police force. I thought that they worked for the people, but I now have really serious doubts. Come on, let's go. We've got a ferry to catch.'

There's one thing about Ada, besides all of her other qualities which I've come to discover, and it's that she has so much energy. As soon as something comes into her head, she's on it, like a cat on a mouse, and off she goes dragging me along like a reluctant tortoise. Well, not so much the tortoise at that time. My shell hadn't gotten quite that thick. More like a snail, I would say.

This time she had decided that we should get to the mainland, catch the bus to the Southampton ferry and then telephone our contact from Ryde once we were on the Isle of Wight.

It all went perfectly. Mr Puttick offered us rooms for the night, but we had become so attached to each other that we opted for just one.

'Saves on the linen,' Ada joked, but it failed to get any kind of response. I don't think Mr Puttick had any views on that score.

We had told our host at the bed and breakfast that we were going to stay one night or possibly two in Southampton, which seemed to please her. Apparently, our booking was during her off-season when she normally took a break, so our short stay was just fine with her.

Chapter 12

Dusk was setting on the Surrey Quays, the murky water losing its lustre except in spots where streetlights cast eerie luminescent mirror images. Occasionally, a chill wind cut across the secretary's face like the slash of a knife, his hand shaking as he brought a cigarette to his lips. *I should've chosen a more sheltered location*, he thought to himself. But the shadowy obscurity and deserted walkways provided the perfect cover for his rendezvous.

The man walking his bicycle calmly approached him. 'Got a light, mate?'

As the Secretary lit the man's cigarette, he was able to confirm his identity. 'It's damn cold, Basilisk. Tell me what you've got.'

'Thanks to your lovely contact, I found out that there have been in-depth inquiries conducted by Adam and Eve's solicitors, namely Dick Robely and Joseph Puttick. Puttick in particular has some close, high-ranking connections in MI6, so it would behove us to be very careful with him.

'Adam the heir has been a recluse, homeless for years, and there's no information regarding his exact whereabouts for the past four decades. He seems to be quite naïve and simple so taking over the lands and property would have been easy had it not been for Eve butting in. And that's not all. I think that you'll find this most interesting.

'Eve and her husband, George, were radical members of an extremist group called Radix, which targeted what they perceived to be corrupt politicians and law enforcement officials. Part of the group focused on vocally addressing environmental and wildlife protection, which sought to ban hunting and certain weapons altogether. I understand that you own land near Eve's farmhouse which is used by hunters for a fee.'

The Secretary flicked his cigarette into the turbid water and slipped his gloved hand into his jacket pocket. 'Yes. Those bastards had been a thorn in my side for years.'

'Anyway, there are notes at MI6 that George may have been involved in an assassination attempt but it could never be proven. Both Eve and George have criminal records and short jail times for unlawful radical acts.'

Numbness caused by the now freezing cold made standing still impossible. Shifting his feet from side to side, the Secretary mumbled, 'I'm well aware of those two and the troubles they've caused. I'm sure you're now also aware that the husband succumbed to a dreadful poison that wasn't discovered until he was gone. Sometimes it's the only way to silence an agitator.

'I've got a strong feeling that Adam and Eve and their cohorts are going to find ways to challenge us and there'll be no stopping them when they find out why we have such a strong interest in acquiring the land. We need to engage our contracted hitmen to eliminate the whole lot, but before we do that, I need you to find out how much they know and their exact plans. Keep me abreast of what they're up to and who's involved.'

'Will do. By the way, any chance you could arrange a social connection with the lovely Anemone?'

'Focus on what I've asked you to do! This is no time for fun and frolic!' The Secretary stiffly walked away leaving Basilisk feeling sorry he had asked.

Chapter 13

Joseph Puttick was a bit of a surprise. I was expecting to see an elderly man in a cardigan, carpet slippers and possibly smoking a pipe. I had always imagined retired professionals in that manner. What we saw was more of a curiosity than a retiree. He was a lot younger than we suspected, around fifty, a beret-wearing, Gauloises-smoking, bearded man dedicated to the growing of onions. He also liked wine, his own, which I was sure he had made with the addition of a little garlic. Strange stuff!

He was a perfect host, to say the least, and as soon as we had eaten, he cleared the dishes himself and went right to the matter at hand. 'Right, so tell me about this dog-fouling litigation.'

Ada's jaw dropped, and I looked at both of them in complete astonishment. Suddenly, Joseph roared with laughter!

'If only you two could see your faces. Oh, my goodness! Dick always used to have a go at me for doing that. Well, first of all, I'm glad that you are here. You can stay as long as you like. Actually, it's quite convenient for me to have you two on tap, so to speak.

'Now about Dick. He called me the day before the police took him in. They want to charge him as an accessory to murder and I understand that he is now being held. I don't think that they can hold him for any more than another day or so. He thinks that when you and he dined at his club, which I hasten to add is strictly members and guests only, someone saw you and decided to break the code. When Dick is released, someone will be thrown out, not only of the club but out of the legal profession as well. Dick knows the law, and he knows full well that the police are doing something outside the law. When this all blows up, there's going to be a lot of red faces and heads rolling.

'Shame about Oscar, though. He was a terrific bloke. I'm really going to miss him. He was so full of enthusiasm, ready for anything. I'm not sure who got him. I can't see Special Branch being quite so public, but the constabulary was very quick to call him a druggie. I must say, there's so much bad news here. I don't quite know who's pulling the strings. Thinking about it now, I don't believe Special Branch is actually involved in this at all. It's even too dirty for them.

'Right! I've had my turn, now what about you two? What have you been doing and, by the way, what actually happened up at your farmhouse, Ada? Dick couldn't tell me on the phone for obvious reasons, but I'd love to know.' Ada explained the whole story to Joseph, who listened intently.

'Well, that all seems to fit in with what I've been hearing down here. Eddie, don't know if you're aware, but you are a very rich man now. Your twin brother returned to the UK after his adoptive father died. Ernest didn't know it at the time, but the old man, Lisle Warren, had accrued several parcels of land and a few houses through the deaths of his relatives around Southampton. It seems that they had all done quite well in their time, and so Lisle became quite well off. That was then. Ernest's own wife passed away some years ago, cancer, I think. When he returned three years ago with his daughter, Marina, he was surprised to see what he had inherited. He tried to find you, but all of his enquiries failed to trace you, which under the present circumstances, was a damned good thing.

'I've got a map of the area and I've drawn out precisely what you've got, including the patch that is causing all the problems. I'll show you.'

Quite seriously, for me to look at a map and know what I was looking at would be a fat chance. To me it looked like blue for the sea, green for the green spaces and the rest, congestion. I actually began to feel a little sick, you know, that deep depressed feeling in the pit of one's stomach. Did I really want all this land that Joseph wanted me to look at? Ada was quite excited, however. She'll never change.

'Eddie, look at this! The land close to the coast. It's all yours! And there's a footpath that runs right through it. We'll have to go for a walk tomorrow and take a look. What do you think?'

What could I say but agree.

'Joseph?' I queried, 'What caused Ernest, Marina and Oscar to die?'

'Simple ... rhodium! There isn't a lot there, so I've heard, but what there is would be worth more than enough to cover a small part of the national debt. There are so few deposits around the world. It's a very rare metal.'

'I'm sorry,' I said, 'but what on earth is rhodium?'

'My goodness, Eddie! It's only the most valuable metal in the world!'

'More than gold?' Ada inquired.

'A lot more than gold! And that is the whole problem for you two. There are some nasty people out there, as you know. And they will not stop until they've either killed you and/or each other. So, be warned, think before you move. Try not to attract attention.'

My head was spinning. I had never visualised wealth. I had never needed it. At that moment, I didn't know what to say or do. 'Ada,' I said, 'Everything's up to you now. You can have it all if you want.'

'No thanks, Eddie. It's sounds too much like a poisoned chalice. We'll sort all this out one way or another. It'll all work out in the end, I'm sure.'

***

Joseph was a great source of local information. He seemed to have a friend in almost every department, whether council, police, or government. Any rumour he stumbled over would be immediately investigated for its source.

'We have a network, you see, in which we can pass, usually anonymously, information relating to almost any subject, whether environmental or industrial, personal or public. A stray word in a queue, wherever it might be, can be picked up, traced, and utilised to maintain the democratic principle that most of us enjoy.

'I can give you an example distantly associated with your present dilemma inasmuch that one of the same players is involved. It concerned a clever chap in Hastings just before the war who invented the first workable, environmentally friendly alternative to the internal combustion engine. It was operated by some kind of fuel cell. I don't know the full details, but by 1947 he was dead, or should I say he was eliminated by a major oil conglomerate and the diagrams and drawings disappeared before they could be patented.

'I can assure you that not too many people followed his example for many a year. What's worse, these people can buy justice from almost any court in our glorious land. We all have to know how and when to vanish, don't we, Ada? From what Dick has said, you're pretty good at that,' Joseph added with a smile.

Ada had been looking at the map, and I could see that she had missed much of what had been said. 'Is the land north or south of the M27? I can't make head nor tail of this.'

'It's both, Ada. It's actually several small parcels fairly close together. Here, I'll show you.' Joseph pointed to a small section near the coast, a little to the west of Stubbington.

'It's not very big, but it's worth its weight in gold, or should I say rhodium. The rest is scattered around. Pointing to the map, he said, 'Look here and here. Other bits are here and another couple of plots and the main one just over there. Tell me, are you going to stay in this area or do you intend to go back to Yorkshire?'

I looked at Ada. I could see what she would rather do.

I answered for both of us. 'I think we would go back, given the chance. There's no space here, is there, Ada? No tranquillity, just too much traffic and too many people. It's not so bad on the island here, but back there, I can't think how people live like that.'

Ada looked pleased, 'We've got the farmhouse, you see, near a small river, not too much land but enough to grow our vegetables for the year. And then, of course, now that Eddie's with me, we can get a couple of goats for milk and maybe rescue a donkey.'

This was the first time that Ada had included me in her future. It was a terrific sensation, a feeling of belonging, being fixed, no longer just passing through.

'And a couple of cats!' I added.

***

The late afternoon shadows had long gone and the darkness outside was only alleviated by the lights from the mainland glinting on the tireless waves that washed the shore just below Joseph's house.

'Wine time!' Joseph jumped up from his seat, and like a man in a hurry, he strode across the room to an old blond-oak sideboard.

'Bought this in a sale a few years ago, twenty quid, serves a treat as a wine cupboard. This particular wine I made three years ago, autumn wine, blackberry and elderberry. It serves well enough as a burgundy, but with a bit of extra body.'

It was a good, strong wine but it definitely had a curious, though not too unpleasant, hint of garlic. I'd heard that some old people used to use garlic as a cleansing medicine and I wondered whether Joseph used a similar product to sterilise his bottles, but I didn't ask. I soon got used to it and so did Ada. I think Joseph was immune.

'Can I make a suggestion?' Joseph looked serious. 'If you go back to the north, would you like me to sell your other holdings down here for you? The four houses would always provide you an income but would be difficult for you to maintain from so far away. The thing is that neither of you have any immediate families, have you, so there is no one who would benefit from such a holding. But if you've got some cash in the bank, then you can do what you want with it while you're fit and able. Think about it. There's no hurry.

'I'm seeing Ernest and Marina's solicitors tomorrow to confirm your identity, Eddie, and progress your inheritance. The sooner that patch by the coast is in your name, the better. Would you sell it, given the right offer?'

'What would you do?' I asked.

'That's a difficult one. The fact that both parties are up to their necks in murder, I think I'd try to gather a consortium of professional metallurgists to extract the minerals, if you wanted to, that is. Under those circumstances, you could share the load amongst several people and each could own part of the holding for a nominal price. Okay, so the production of the rhodium would not be immediate but at least it would all be out of reach of those bastards, whoever they are. What's more, it would give you the chance to nail the people who are guilty of murder. But it's only a thought.

'That reminds me, there's a new face on the block. His name is Wragge, an ex-policeman from Sussex. It's been noted that he's still trying to pass himself off as a detective sergeant and has been asking a lot of questions about Marina's inheritance and if anyone is trying to claim it. It seems he doesn't know about you being in the area yet, or maybe he does and is trying to flush you out. So be very careful. From what I can gather, he's got a connection to a Russian businessman, so we know what he's about. By the way, my notion is that he was responsible for killing Marina. I just have a feeling about it.

'You know, after years in this profession, one gets a gut feeling about certain criminal types. He's got a history of corruption. One thing most of them forget is that when they tread on a colleague for whatever reason, that colleague will do anything to get even. So, at the moment, there is a mass of intelligence floating around him and all his dirty dealings. If we don't get him, I'm sure somebody else will.'

There was plenty there for Ada and me to mull over. It was difficult for both of us to visualise how Joseph could have become so involved in our case so that he knew more of it than we did. Joseph rose, gathered his breath, and declared that he was about to prepare the evening meal. Ada offered to help but he declined, saying that we had plenty to think about. He did, however, pour out another glass of his elixir which appeared to clarify our thoughts, or so it seemed.

Thus, another day had ended even more confusing than the previous one.

Chapter 14

The following day, Ada and I decided to take the ferry back to Southampton. The idea was for me to look up some of the places that I remembered from earlier days when I was at the orphanage.

Sure enough, the black cross which marked the entrance to St Michael was still there, but there was nothing to be seen of the home. Instead, a four-storey office block stood in its place, which actually looked worse than the old home. Well, that's what I thought, anyway.

'Bearing in mind that you spent much of your childhood and teens in a home, how is it that you have such a liking for cats? Was there one at St Michael or what?' Ada asked me as we wandered through the interminable maze of streets, many of which I had no recollection of whatsoever. So many things had changed.

'It all started when I was about seventeen. We were hiding out in a derelict hotel, one of the many that had never been sorted out after the war, you know, bomb damage and so on. It was the same all along the south coast in those days. Anyway, there were a couple of kitties in the area, and I always managed to find something to give them to eat. Well, I think that the word got out between them because within three weeks there were about six, then ten and so it went. They would even follow me down the street.

'I loved them all and spent most of the day trying to find enough scraps to make their lives a little bit easier. When we were finally kicked out by the police, I managed to get a cat refuge to take them on. It took us around two weeks to catch them all with the police trying to obstruct us at every move. I don't know what was wrong with them. They didn't seem to have any compassion.

'From what we were told, it was the cats that got us thrown out. There was an old man a couple of doors along the road who we thought was either Russian or Polish. He had four or five little dogs, and we used to call him Pavlov. Unfortunately, one day when the cats got a bit hungry, they set upon one of the dogs when it was alone in the street. They then dragged it back to the squat and ate the poor thing when we weren't there. So Pavlov called the police. Of course, the cats denied any knowledge of it, but nonetheless the police believed him rather than the cats, and they threw us all out. And that's why I am so fond of cats. It was like being one of them, struggling to survive.'

'Surely they didn't really catch the dog and eat it!' Ada thought I was joking.

'Yes. We found bits and pieces of it upstairs in one of the attic rooms. Bits of fur and bones and most of its head. That was the part that they couldn't break up, I suppose.'

Ada looked horrified. 'Eddie, that is dreadful!'

We were quiet for a while and Ada kept looking at me sort of sideways on. It was really quite funny, and eventually I had to sit down on a bench and laugh. It was just too much.

We found all four houses that Ernest had inherited, including the one in which he had been living and which had been empty since his death. Marina had a flat in Portsmouth that she rented overlooking the sea, but we didn't visit that. There was nothing spectacular about any of the properties but, of course, they all represented wealth. It was really strange. On the one hand there was me, penniless, and on the other hand my twin, the recipient of what I would call a fortune. Now it was mine, or was just about to be.

***

The following day, we decided to visit the rest of the estate. In the early morning, we settled the bill at our Hayling

Island accommodation and returned the bike to the Isle of Wight.

Joseph had done well and told us that everything was sorted out and that all we had to do was wait for the probate to be finalised. He said that it would probably take a few months, which put us in a rather difficult position. It's not that we were impatient. Neither of us was desperate for wealth. It was more a case of ducking and diving to keep out of sight and out of danger.

Joseph suggested that I should cut my hair, grow a beard, and wear a hat. It might have been sensible, but I didn't have the right sort of walk to take on a new persona. When one has been, let's say, a traveller on the highways and byways, one develops a definite sort of amble, always lopsided with a positive lurch to the left. It doesn't go well with all that modern stuff. It's almost like buying special scissors to get rid of one's nose hair.

Once we got back on the bike, we thought it might be best to take the back roads, off the usual run, and it wasn't long before we were cruising along the land that so many people were keen to own. I don't know much about the law, but I assumed that there was going to be a whole list of shortcuts that certain legal individuals were going to use to grab the land. That sort of thing doesn't give one much faith in the law, does it?

There wasn't much to see except one thing which was rather striking: a high security fence with notices every fifty metres, 'Keep Out — Private Land'. To cap it all, a public footpath marker had been wrenched out of the ground and left lying at the side of the bank.

Ada slowed right down as we passed until we could see a gateway into the plot. Both of us noticed the security camera poised over the entrance, and she gathered speed in an attempt to avert attention. It seemed to work. The camera didn't move to follow us and so, having seen enough for the day, we returned just in time to catch the five o'clock ferry back to the island. We had left the bike in a secure parking area on the mainland and took a taxi back to Joseph's.

***

For someone who normally appeared bright and breezy, it was a little foreboding to find Joseph's greeting a little less than welcoming.

'I'm glad you're back,' he said as we entered the house. 'Bad news, I'm afraid. Dick's been charged as an accessory to murder, the victim being Marina. There is now a nationwide hunt for you, Eddie, for murder and you, Ada, for conspiracy. You need some good allies and quick! I'm at a bit of a loss as to what to suggest. There aren't too many places to hide round here.'

'Do you know Diana Plowright?' Ada asked. 'She and George used to get on like a house on fire. Like minds. I never suspected there was anything else. She used to be a top dog in the Mersey police. I think she might be able to help.'

'This is quite a coincidence. Ada, I hate to tell you, but she's the one who's heading the enquiry. She's the one who had Dick arrested.' Joseph looked totally bemused.

'Well, if she's lifted Dick, there must have been a good reason. It must have been to get him out of harm's way. Give her a ring and ask her why he's involved. Tell her that you're an old colleague of his and that you want to represent him in the case, whatever it is. She might be cagey at first, so tell her that you knew my husband, George. She'll probably open up then.'

I sat there and watched these two people, who I didn't know existed a couple of months before, putting their lives on the line for me. It really didn't make any sense. There I was, more or less a recluse, keeping out of the way of society, then suddenly there are all these people, some dead, others obviously going to die. For what? It just didn't seem right! I had to say something and make it right.

'This is all my fault. I should have left Marina where she was and gone away from the moor, but because I didn't, so many people are dead, and there's a possibility that we could all end up in prison. So why don't I go to the police and tell them that I killed Marina and that I tricked everybody else into helping me. Then it would all be over and you could carry on without the worry of looking after me.'

Ada was horrified. I thought to myself, what have I said? She had a look on her face as if I had hit her with a rock.

'Is that all I'm worth to you, Eddie?' There was venom in her eyes. 'How dare you even suggest that we abandon this, and for you to abandon me after all we've been through together. Why do you think I'm here? Come on, tell me! Why am I here?'

There were two possible answers to her question. One was that she wanted a share in the wealth that would be available if we got through the situation alive. The other one was that she really cared for me.

'I'm sorry,' I said, but I could hardly look her in the face. 'It's the second thing.'

'What do you mean, the second thing?' She was clearly angry.

'That you really care for me.'

'So, the first thing is...? Don't tell me! God, Eddie, you could drive me insane with that sort of rubbish. Do you think for one moment that I am in the least bit interested in what you might inherit? Do you want me to go home now and leave you to get on with your silly ideas?'

She looked at me with such an expression, a cross between anger and compassion. What could I say? I felt absolutely awful. Joseph had left the room, and I certainly couldn't blame him for that, but it made me realise that I needed to regard my relationship with Ada as real and not as some passing adventure.

'I'm so sorry, Ada. I've never had a relationship before, not a proper relationship, and I have difficulty imagining that there is anything in me that is worthy of your affection. Just look at me. I've never had a personality. It's kind of a missing part. But being with you is like growing into something much more complicated, and it's not always so easy for me to adjust to it.

'Now with all this trouble I've caused, I find it hard to imagine that you would stick by me regardless of anything that can possibly happen. The thing is, Ada, that I don't want to live without you, but at the same time, I can't believe that you could possibly feel the same for me. You are so resourceful. You have answers to almost everything, and here I am, a complete dunderhead when it comes to making decisions and choosing the right path.'

'Eddie, I'm not going to argue. You are a complete dunderhead, whatever that is, but all this is not your fault. There are some really bad people out there and it is them, not you, who are to blame for what has happened. Remember, you found Marina. It was an extraordinary coincidence. Call it fate that you found her, but it wasn't you who killed her and left her body in a place that you called your own.

'Yes, I am more than fond of you, Eddie. You are really very precious to me, and what's more, this entanglement has given me a purpose. I haven't had such a lift in my spirits since George tried to blow up the prime minister, but that's another story.

'Eddie, I'm going to say it now and don't you ever doubt it again. I love you. Now that was very hard for me to say, so don't expect to hear it again. Okay?'

She stepped right up to me and gave me a really big hug and a quick peck on the lips. I'll say one thing about that: it certainly brought the colour back to my cheeks.

'Phew, Ada, that was really nice! Look, I really am sorry. I promise I will never doubt you again, not that I really doubted you, anyway. It was more like doubting myself. Thank you. You've made me feel so accepted and I suppose safe for the first time in a very long time. A lifetime, in fact.'

Joseph returned and sheepishly looked at us.

'Everything resolved?' He smiled. 'Good, we can move on now, can't we. Anyway, things aren't as bad as I thought, thanks to you, Ada. I have just got hold of Diana Plowright. She was very cautious at first, but I sensed that someone was in her office. Anyway, just as you suspected, Dick has been put out of harm's way. She has asked me to call her in the future on her mobile. It's obvious she knows what's going on. By the way, I don't know how she knew, but she said, "Give my love to Ada. It would be nice to see her again." I pretended that I didn't know where you were, but I think that she has Dick's confidence.'

'I hope she doesn't get hurt and has a trustworthy crew she can rely on,' said Ada. 'Have you warned her about Richards?'

'Damn, I forgot! I had better call her back. If she confides in him, we will all be in serious trouble.' Joseph turned and left the room.

While he was gone, I took the opportunity to ask Ada why George had wanted to blow up the prime minister. What she said was so unexpected, it stuck in my mind.

'Eddie, as far as George was concerned, he reckoned that he had a good reason to get rid of the prime minister. He had cost George his job and he was blacklisted, as were the rest of his colleagues. They had been working on a perpetual motion machine, something like a waterwheel, using compressed hydrogen balanced against ballast. They reckoned that if they could get perfect accuracy in the compression of the hydrogen, they could manufacture generators that produced low-cost electricity on a huge scale. In fact, if they had been able to complete the research, there would've been none of this reliance on fossil energy. The prime minister knew that, so he ended the research, and anyone involved in the work was made redundant and could never get a job in the industry again.

'George decided it was time for him to go, so he followed him wherever he went, and guess what? George discovered that the prime minister was having an affair with a dog-breeder from Huddersfield. He and this woman would go to a motel every other Wednesday. George rigged up a device in the loo cistern in the room that they always occupied.

'Unfortunately, the Falklands war broke out and the two of them never turned up. Before George had a chance to retrieve the object, a drug pusher hired the room and discovered the bomb when he tried to hide his stash of cocaine. The pusher ran for it without paying the hotel bill. The police were called; the guy was caught, charged with drug offences and terrorism, was found guilty, and is probably still serving time. There was nothing George could do without admitting his part in the affair. So that's it. And then George died three years later. God only knows if the prime minister was actually having an affair or if they were involved in some sort of covert MI5 meetings, which is more than likely. It's like a disease being a politician. I'm sure there were some who knew what was going on, but the truth never came out.'

I had a few more questions, but at that moment Joseph came back looking mighty pleased. 'Dick had already alerted her, so she has sent Richards on a fool's errand to Belgium for a joint investigation into MEPs' expense frauds. She was asked to find volunteers, and she could see quite clearly that Richards was looking for a way out, so she gave him the chance. Anyway, it should keep him out of the picture for several months, though it won't help him much if we can't get everything sorted out by the time he returns. She said that she will keep me informed if anything untoward turns up.

'Also, she wants you both to know that you have got to get things moving because she can only stall the murder enquiry for a short while. She knows that you are in the south but doesn't want to know any more than that for the moment. Wragge must not set eyes on you. She said that he is really bad news but that she can't find enough evidence to put him behind bars. She believes someone is covering his steps wherever and whatever he gets involved in. Papers apparently disappear along with evidence and nobody knows anything.

'There's an obvious sense of fear that shows itself every time his name is mentioned. I wonder who's running him. It must be someone with a lot of power and a hand in a huge pot of money. Personally, I think we are probably looking at a high-ranking government official, but which one?'

The evening carried on in much the same vein until we all eventually went off to bed.

I was just dozing off when Ada gave me a nudge with her elbow. 'Eddie, quiet. Don't speak. Now listen to me, not a word to Joseph.' She whispered. 'We might need these very soon for our own protection.'

I could feel something cold and hard being pressed into my hand. I guessed what it was but I couldn't think how Ada had kept the existence of it quiet for so long.

'It's only a .22 pistol but at close range it will still make a nasty little hole.'

'Ada, where am I going to put it so it can't be seen?'

'Put it under your pillow for the moment, and I'll show you how to hide it in the morning. I've got one as well.'

'George again?' I queried.

'Yes, George again. Eddie, the trigger is a bit light so handle it with care. I've got a feeling that before long we might just have another night visitor.'

'Oh, I hope not!' Then after a pause, 'Ada, there's so much about your life that I don't know. I'm just curious about a few things. If you don't care to talk about it, then it's okay.'

'Eddie, we're in a relationship now and I have no problem telling you what you want to know. Ask away.'

'Well, you seem to know a lot about guns and making explosives. That's very unusual for a woman to know. And what happened to George? You mentioned that he died unexpectedly.'

Ada hesitated for a moment, then took a deep breath. 'Eddie, I hope that what I'm about to tell you doesn't change anything between us.'

'It's okay, Ada. I want to know.'

'George and I met when we were members of an underground radical group that worked to expose shady politicians and police corruption. We found that the two often conspired to embezzle funds at the expense of the citizens they're supposed to serve and protect. They stopped at nothing in their quest for the almighty dollar, including blackmail, fraud, destruction of our environment and wildlife, even murder. And who was fighting for the ordinary citizen? No one. That is, until our group came along and decided to fight fire with fire. It seemed to be the only way.

'I've already told you that George had been an engineer of sorts, and he taught me all that he knew about making weapons and explosives from raw materials. Soon we were made targets by unscrupulous government officials as we became more vocal and militant. That's when he decided to create a hideaway in the cave as we knew that, at some point, they would come for us. Some of us were imprisoned, including George and me when we became careless and rode into town to attend a demonstration. Some lost their lives to the cause.

'One day George came home after a meeting at a local café feeling quite sick and not himself. He refused to get help thinking he had caught a virus that would soon pass with rest. I tried to nurse him back to health, but by the third day, he was in agonising pain and unable to keep anything down. I rushed him to the hospital, but by the end of the day, he was gone.

'Sadly, the organisation disbanded due to the pressure put upon us by infiltrators and instigators who created discord between us. We no longer knew who to trust.

'I was tired of fighting and just wanted some peace back in my life but I never abandoned my beliefs and convictions, never turned my back on anyone who needed my help. And then you came into my life and gave me a renewed purpose for being.' She held my hand and said, 'And I thank you for that.'

'Ada, I appreciate your honesty. Your courage gives me such strength and your acceptance of me as I am is something I've never felt from anyone. There's nothing to worry about. None of it changes what I think of you.'

We looked into each other's eyes, and for the first time in my life, I felt a stirring in my soul, an astonishing oneness with another human being, much like I had first felt with Marina, except that now this woman was alive and she was real. Ada slowly leaned into me and kissed me, soft and sweet. Then I held her hoping that she could feel what was in my heart but couldn't say. It was all so new to me that I didn't even know how to explain it to myself. Eventually we fell asleep in each other's arms.

Chapter 15

The following morning, I stuck the gun Ada had given to me in the top of my trousers just to the left of my belt buckle before we went down to the kitchen for breakfast. It wasn't that comfortable despite being quite small and I was a little worried I might shoot my private bits off if I moved too quickly. To give myself a little peace of mind, I placed it on the table as we settled down to eat. It was just as we had finished that Ada heard someone approaching.

'Eddie, put it away, quick. Joseph is coming!'

What was always nice about Joseph was his breeziness. No matter what the problem might be, he was always ready with a smile.

'Hello, you two. Good breakfast, yes? I've spoken with Tom this morning, who was able to gather some information for us, though not much more than what we already know. Unfortunately, the identity of specific individuals who are vying for your land has been redacted from available documents. No matter. We have a pretty good idea of who might be involved. I've asked him to try and gather intelligence on what our main suspect is up to but, as he pointed out, asking too many questions could put him in a precarious position. We just need to keep our ears and eyes open.

'Look here, we need to move today and get this business into a proper perspective. I'm picking up the keys to Ernest's house this morning on the mainland, so I think you should come with me as prospective buyers. That means that you should continue using the Grantham name. Have you got any hiking gear? I think it might be interesting for you to take a good look at what you own.

'What I'll do in a minute is phone a few old friends, enough to form a party, that way you won't look out of place when and if we meet any opposition. There are a couple of footpaths that run through the land, and if we come across any resistance, we can cause a bit of a ruck. That'll aggravate them, I'm sure.'

***

Everything went as planned. I found Ernest's house strange. There were photos of him and his wife and of her with Marina as a little girl, but there was nothing that demonstrated a full life lived in that house. We didn't stay long, and by half past twelve, Ada and I had to remind Joseph that it was nearly lunchtime.

At 2.30 pm, we were waiting for the other 'hikers' down at the ferry port terminal. One of Joseph's friends had access to a minibus which was emblazoned with the emblem of a local charity. It was certainly a good cover. Half an hour later, we were on the track. Midway through our ramble, we found ourselves standing in front of a high metal gate blocking our path with a huge notice in large red capitals: NO ADMITTANCE — PRIVATE LAND.

Joseph gave the gate a good shaking, and we could see the security camera swing round to focus on our merry band. Joseph shouted towards the camera, 'This is a public right of way. You've got no business putting up a gate here. We demand access to continue our walk.'

Ada stood close to me and whispered, 'This could be interesting,' and she wasn't wrong. About thirty metres from the gate was a glorified B & Q garden shed from which a rather large, unkempt individual emerged.

'Clear off!' the lummox shouted. 'Go on, bugger off, the lot of you before I call my boss.'

Joseph shouted back, 'Go on, call him. I dare you! Do that and I'll call the police. Open this gate at once, you pathetic turd!'

That really did it. The man stormed over, red-faced and with blood in his eyes. Opening the gate, he yelled, 'Who are you calling a turd!'

'You!' returned Joseph. 'We demand access to this pathway. You have no legal right whatsoever to close it!'

'So you're the brains, are you? If you weren't so bloody old, I'd have given you one by now!'

What I have come to love about rebellion is that it's nearly always justified. So when a fair-sized stone flew through the air and caught the lummox fair and square on top of his head, the stakes were immediately raised to danger level. The man raised himself from the ground with a trickle of blood running down behind his right ear, his dirty beige ponytail flipping from side to side as he staggered towards us.

He still thought that he was in control, being bigger than any two of us. He raised his mobile to his bloody ear when Maureen Dickens jabbed him in the front part of his jeans with one of her Nordic walking sticks. He didn't like that too much and fell down again with a mighty groan. For a few minutes, it all seemed to be over. Meredith, who the others called Merry, was cussing like a trooper and continued to beat him with a fallen branch every time he tried to get up.

It was at that point that a black Range Rover appeared. Two men climbed out and raised shotguns at our little group. They were followed by a small raggedy sort of man with a nasty rodentine nose who positioned himself between the other two. Ada pulled her hat lower over her eyes.

'Is he close enough for me to shoot him, do you think?' I asked.

'Yes and no. Not this time, Eddie. Don't let him see your face.'

It was Wragge, obviously now the man in charge. 'Leave my man alone or it'll be the last thing any of you will ever do!'

Joseph stood forward. 'We demand access to the footpath.'

'Too bad!' came the reply 'You'd better go home and play with your toys, you stupid old farts.'

It was almost a stalemate. They thought that they had all the high cards and slowly moved forward to ensure that we backed off.

Joseph had obviously kept his hand close to his chest on this occasion. Neither Ada nor I had anticipated what happened next. One of the two heavies suddenly screamed and dropped to the ground holding his head. We could see blood running through his fingers and down his face, soaking his blue denim jacket to a dense purple colour. For a second, Wragge looked worried.

Out of nowhere, a piece of wood cartwheeled through the air and caught the other henchman across the side of his head. He went down as well, but this time in silence. Wragge made off towards the Range Rover, but not quickly enough. He went down about five paces from the vehicle with his right arm stretched out in front of him. Joseph put his foot on the man's back, holding him down.

'Now, listen to me, Wragge. Yes, I know who you are. My advice to you now is go back to Sussex and don't come anywhere near here again because I know who you work for and I'm going to tell him that there is a bigger man than him laying claim to this land. So, go while you still can. Take these oafs with you and don't ever dare to come back.'

Hardly had Joseph finished his sentence when we all heard a heavy motor rumbling close by. My immediate thought was that we were about to be in some even greater danger, but Joseph turned to us and waved his hands in a downward motion. 'It's okay, you lot! Just a little help from a friend.'

The JCB made very short work of the gate and much of the surrounding fencing before turning away to demolish the shed.

The excavator disappeared along the path just as unexpectedly as it had arrived.

Wragge was still on the ground with his arms wrapped over his head for fear of being crushed by the machine. Joseph gave him a hefty kick in the thigh which sent Wragge rolling over. I could see, at that point, something that Joseph couldn't. Wragge was reaching for a small revolver from a holster just above his shoe.

I shouted, 'Joseph! Look out!' A shot rang out. It was all over in a split second. As Wragge flopped down, he had a look of total disbelief. Then he passed out.

Joseph turned to me, just as surprised. 'Thanks, Eddie!'

I noticed Ada slip her little pistol back into her bag, smoke still wisping from the barrel. I looked down at my hand. Mine was doing the same thing, the barrel still warm. Indeed, we had shot Wragge together at the very same instant when we both saw what he was about to do.

Joseph tore Wragge's shirt open, blood oozing from the gunshot wounds. There were two small holes in his upper right chest no more than a centimetre apart.

'I don't know what you've got there, Eddie, but it's an interesting gadget, that's for sure! Come on, you lot. Let's finish our walk. He's not badly hurt. He'll probably get himself to hospital when he comes to. We never saw a thing, did we? '

***

Later that evening, as we mulled over the day's events, I asked Joseph who the people were that accompanied us during the hike.

'They call themselves the Wingeing Ninjas on account of a couple of them always moaning about something or other. They are all close friends and all one-time clients of mine. They all have something in common, and that is that they have all been cheated on by either politicians or local government councillors, usually through some underhanded dealing over property. Because of that, they were happy to come with us today.

'Besides, some three years ago, I organised for them a self-defence class which has given them a great deal of self-confidence. By and large, they are a bunch of tough old cookies, ready to have a go at almost anything as long as it involves trouble. Mind you, they know how to keep quiet, so don't worry about the pistol. By the way, what is that? Is it double-barrelled or something?'

I looked at Ada, who was watching me closely. She nodded. I had the thing stuffed inside the waist band of my trousers and had totally forgotten it was there. It was one of those things that, being steel, had taken up my body heat and was tucked away in such a position that I was totally unaware that I still had it with me. Still warm, I handed it to Joseph.

'But it's only got one barrel, not two! I don't understand. There was only one shot fired. This thing is only a single-shot gun, so how did Wragge end up with two holes in his chest?'

Ada opened her bag and gave Joseph the other one. He sniffed the barrel.

'Oh, I see! Firing in unison. Very funny. I don't believe you two!' He handed back the weapons and fell back in his chair laughing.

'I'm going to check tomorrow to see if anybody has turned up in casualty with gunshot wounds. I've got a good friend in Southampton General who hears a lot of gossip. So it could be interesting. Anyway, we've put a hornet into the hive, so let's see what those busy little bees do now!'

Chapter 16

Living rough taught me one simple thing: to wake up in the morning and find that one is still alive and not covered in urine from a passing drunk, that is a real bonus. That is basically why I chose to move into the countryside. It's not that there is a more considerate class of people in the countryside, but there's just less of the riffraff. So to be alive, and now happy to be so, is a great improvement over what I had thought was a kind of terminal ailment, a withering inevitably leading to death somewhere by the side of a road or in a ditch. I don't know how I really found myself in that situation. I suppose it was all engendered by the treatment I received at St Michael and the fact that my twin brother was sent away from me. That, and being constantly told that I was of no use to society, was enough to send me straight into a decline.

Ada was my rescuer, and now my life was not only changed, but had become so intriguing. I never expected to be involved in such an adventure. Having never had money, the idea of having loads of it was totally alien to me. What the hell would I do with it? Okay, we all have dreams, but mine have never included wealth. I must say, though, not having to search the hedgerows for food will be an experience all its own. I like that part. It makes life so much more bearable.

***

Joseph was out when we got up. We were both worried about where he might've gone and any possible fallout from the previous day, until he returned at midday.

'Busy morning, I'm afraid. I should have left you a note. Firstly, I checked the site of our little altercation and found that there was no sign of the infamous four. Then I checked with my contact in Southampton General. Apparently, there was a call for a surgeon from a private clinic at around eight last night, but when the A&E clerk asked what the problem was, the caller hung up. My guess is that somehow they were able to contact a confidential surgeon for treatment. I doubt that Wragge has succumbed to his wounds, so we may not have heard the last of him yet.

'I hope Wragge took my advice, but I doubt he will. I think it will end badly for him. He has made too many mistakes to be forgiven and may be seen as a liability. But that's his problem to sort out, not ours. Our next step is to give his boss a clip around the ears.'

'Who is he working for? It's become so complicated that I'm actually having trouble keeping up,' I queried.

'Oh, Eddie, you'll catch on soon enough. You just need to understand how the system works. Tell him, Ada!'

'Eddie, listen to me. Who controls local planning?'

'The local council, I suppose.'

'Correct, but who controls the local council if there is any disagreement?'

'The county council?'

'Yes, but who controls the county council if there is a disagreement with a government policy?'

'The Secretary of State for the Environment? Is that it? Is that what all this is about?'

Joseph and Ada both nodded, but Joseph had more to add.

'Eddie, it's actually worse than that. I have it on good authority that this Secretary of State for the Environment is actually doing very bad things with a certain Russian millionaire. It's funny how power always corrupts. For years this particular person has lived in the half-light and then, suddenly, there he is in a high-ranking position and he has to take the first financial proposition that's offered to him. Not only that, but he has also slipped between the covers with this particular Russian. Not an ordinary everyday Russian millionaire, mind you, but one who has already faced prosecution for corruption within the Soviet prison system, not as a prisoner but as a governor. He's obviously fallen out of favour with quite a few people.

'By the way, you know Merry was a bit wayward yesterday on our little trek. You remember that she lagged behind the rest of us for a while. Well, the thing is, Merry is bit of a magpie, a collector. If something is discarded and she thinks it could be useful, then she will pick it up and carry it off. So what she did yesterday was to gather up the two shotguns and Wragge's gun, raid the Range Rover while our assailants were still immobile, and then rummage through the remains of the shed for ammunition and any other weapons.

'She hid the shotguns in the undergrowth but managed to stuff the rest into her bag. I only know this because she was back at the site this morning. I met her just as she was leaving. She was carrying a cricket bag which looked quite heavy. When I asked what she was up to, she showed me. It was quite a shock. We obviously caught them unawares because what she had collected was such an array of weapons. Altogether, she had four shotguns, two handguns and three grenades plus the ammunition.

'So now the Wingeing Ninjas are fully armed. She told me that she enjoyed yesterday so much that we can rely on her at any time and added that she spoke for the rest of the group. The thing is, we don't want a Southampton shootout, so we may have to involve some other agency to deal with any really big problems. I know a couple of people who owe me a favour, but I'd rather not make the call unless it's critical. Come on, smile, you two!'

Ada burst out laughing. 'You know, Joseph, I'm a north country girl and humour doesn't come easily, but you really do take the biscuit. You and all your buddies are all nuts, but unbelievably good folk. There aren't too many people like you lot in this world. I mean, you haven't asked for a penny in rent. Here we are still breezing through Dick's money. It's almost like living on charity and at the same time gambling. It's wonderful and odd at the same time.'

She was right, of course. Ada is so clear-sighted, she amazes me. She understands which way the wind blows and even knows who's doing the blowing, leaving me way behind struggling to follow even the first bits of whatever it is that she's already tucked away. I sat there dazed by all the complications that the situation was throwing at us. I couldn't imagine Merry firing a shotgun let alone throwing a grenade. I decided to leave everything up to the others in the hope that I could catch up through my exposure to whatever they were doing.

Joseph, in a more serious tone, suggested that we should both join the self-defence/martial arts class to 'tune up,' as he put it. It was a good idea and we would be well placed and in good company with our newfound friends.

It was silly, really. I was born in Southampton, and in a way, I would have liked to have stayed. But my links with the North York Moors and my new love and companion made me wish that none of this stuff had happened and that we could just return to live our lives in peace together. But finding Marina had put us both on a death list. We both understood that, but we also knew that we had to keep on going until the whole thing was resolved one way or another.

***

There was a lull for a while, and with Christmas on the horizon, Ada and I fell into a false sense of security, expecting a peaceful interval until the New Year. But on the 12th of December, someone took a shot at Joseph. Fortunately, he was only slightly wounded, a piece of flesh being ripped from his bicep onto the window of a passing car.

It only served to make him more determined to bring the business to a head. All I thought was that whoever was behind this was just as determined to do away with all of us. I've never been in a situation like this, and it was terrifying. It made me wonder if owning all that land was worth it. Again, I brought up my worries with Ada.

'You know, Eddie, I completely understand your concern. It's a dirty, dangerous business. But it goes beyond getting what is rightfully yours. This government official and his allies are looking at your property and its rare and valuable minerals as a means to fill their pockets and use their proceeds to further control others and their own interests. And they don't care who or what they destroy.

'What's more, think about all you could do with all that land and what it holds. You're such a selfless man and you could, if you wanted to, share your wealth with others who do good deeds for the benefit of mankind. You could turn it into a protected nature reserve for wildlife.

'Our friends are vested in ending the corruption and destruction and are willing to take risks to end the madness. Do you understand now?'

'Yes, I see what you mean.' I suppose it was easier for Ada to make sense of it all since she had dealt with this kind of turmoil before. I had been so far removed from politics and the like, it was harder for me to understand this passion for righting the wrongs. All I knew was that I was at peace with my simple life away from all the chaos. I guess this was a lesson I needed to learn.

***

On the 20th of December, Joseph returned midafternoon, quite happy that he had learned the identity of the madman who had tried to kill him. He clapped his hands and declared, 'Right, that's that sorted. Slow boat to China in chains. I hope somebody finds him before he gets too hungry. The good thing is that they now know who I am and that I mean business. Fortunately, they still don't know what you two look like, except for Messrs Wragge and Richards.'

Ada was a little concerned, though, particularly about Wragge. 'Wragge's going to be a problem, isn't he? Don't you think that it would be a better world without him?'

'I can't disagree, but I'm not too sure if Eddie is ready for such an assignment. He'll need some special training before he tackles that.'

I was horrified. The last thing I'd want to do is go out specifically to kill somebody. It would be okay, I guess, if it was in self-defence, but to go out and deliberately murder somebody ... well, I couldn't possibly do it. Or could I? Suddenly, the thought of disposing of a person who was a real menace, not just to us, but probably to a great many other people too, was worth thinking about ... definitely a consideration. After all, if I didn't do it, someone else would probably have to at some time or another.

The problem was that all these thoughts were not going through my mind very fast. Basically, I'm a slow thinker. I make no bones about it. I take my time to mull things over, but what is worst is that my clockwork brain gives the game away in my facial expressions.

When I looked up, the pair of them were quietly laughing, trying to contain their mirth. But they just couldn't hold it back and collapsed laughing out loud, tears running down their faces, making me feel really bad.

'Oh, we're sorry, Eddie, my love. It was just your face. You went from deep thought to extreme panic, and we knew exactly what you were thinking.' Ada put her arm around me and gave me a hug. I liked that but I felt that I needed to get my own back. Resentment is not a nice feeling!

Joseph could see how things were and softened his amusement. 'Don't worry, old chap. Merry will probably be the one to bump him off. She's mad enough but also remarkably resourceful. Now look, it's just coming up to six and I've got a little surprise for you, both of you, particularly you, Ada.'

We looked at each other puzzled. *What does he mean?*

The doorbell chime made us start. Not only had we not heard it before, but it was also very sharp, not so much an electric ding-dong but more like a church bell with a crack in it.

Joseph opened the door. 'Come in! Spot on for timing!'

And there they were, Dick, Tom, and a woman I had never seen before, but Ada was obviously very pleased to see her. She jumped up and gave the woman a big hug.

'Eddie! This is Diana Plowright.'

I thought to myself, is this a good thing, a senior policewoman being privy to our secret? But I could see that Ada had every confidence in her.

'Diana, this is the notorious murderer, Eddie Dew. Have you got your handcuffs ready?'

Diana put her hand out to greet me but then lunged forward and gripped my arm. I pulled back, confused. 'Murderer, my foot!' she said. 'This lamb wouldn't hurt a fly, let alone kill his own niece.'

Yet there I was a few minutes before, wondering if I could get rid of Wragge. It had all become just too muddled in my head. Not only that, I wasn't quite sure I liked being called a lamb. Just the day before, I had shot someone.

Dick had been holding two large square cartons when he arrived, and then he and Joseph disappeared into the kitchen.

Ada and I shook hands with Tom, who was almost unrecognisable out of his tailored suit and dressed in casual attire. 'What have you been up to, Tom?' Ada inquired.

'No good,' was his quick retort, which made everyone chuckle. 'Actually, I've been working diligently on your case.

What little intel I was able to gather, I shared with Dick and Joseph. I'm sure by now he's clued you in. Where are you both staying these days?'

'Joseph has been kind enough to let us stay here for the time being,' Ada replied.

'Oh, good! He's a great host, but whatever you do, beware of his homemade garlic-wine concoction. It's rancid, but don't tell him I told you so. It'll hurt his feelings.'

'That's a very interesting bracelet, Tom. The blue stones on the serpent's eyes are quite eye-catching,' Ada said admiringly.

'Oh, thank you! It was a gift from a good friend who said the stones are blue opals from Peru. Supposedly they provide emotional healing and clairvoyant abilities, but I don't believe in such things. I fell in love with the unusual design and rarely take it off. It's become my personal statement piece.'

Just then, Joseph walked in. 'Dinner is served!' And there it was, hot and ready to be eaten at once. I must admit, takeaway pizzas can be very agreeable, almost as good as a SpudULike with baked beans and cheese on top.

I had some difficulty understanding what position Diana had in the police force. She was certainly in the upper level of her career, but what department? I did ask her but all she would reply was that she investigated things of which the public was normally unaware.

'It's something to do with corruption in high places,' she said. 'In your case, Eddie, there has been a murder, or should I say murders, and to keep my investigations hidden, I needed you to be the scapegoat. Don't worry. You won't be arrested, but you need to remain as Mr Grantham for the time being.

'You remember Oscar, don't you? He worked for us quite often but he got too close to a certain person. He found out too much, nothing relating to Marina or to your brother, more like pay-offs within the city of London. Too much money floating around there with no real control is a recipe for political corruption, as we have already seen. The trouble is that this government keeps its friends well covered, and it's rare for any of them to be put away. No one dares to touch them.

'Anyway, that's what happened to Oscar. He was a good man, and we all liked him. He worked hard and actually had a conscience. I wonder how much that tip-off was worth and was it paid in cash or with a bullet? That is something we will probably never know.'

'I hold myself to blame,' Dick interrupted. 'I thought the club was a safe place for you two and him to meet, but obviously it wasn't. There must be somebody there who needs to be rooted out, if they're still living, that is.'

'Dick, it might have happened elsewhere. He was doing so many other things. The problem is that now it will be so difficult to find anyone as dedicated to the truth as Oscar. We will nail the lowlife that killed him, and his end will come from an unexpected quarter. You see, our department doesn't take prisoners. If we did, our very existence would become known and we would have to close up shop.

'By the way, that pizza wasn't too bad, was it? It went well with the hint of garlic in your wine, Joseph.' I could see that Diana had a sharp sense of humour.

Tom tittered. 'I see Joseph's magic potion has made the rounds.'

Joseph got up as if to leave, went to the sideboard, and took out another bottle. As he refilled Diana's glass, he muttered with a sarcastic smile, 'This is from an earlier year, a very good year for garlic. Enjoy!'

It's incredible how Joseph had managed it, but no matter what the vintage, the wine always had that subtle hint of garlic. Mind you, by that time we were so accustomed to it that we were always pleased to have another glass.

'What variety of grape do you use for this, Joseph?' We could see that Diana wanted to carry on the amusement.

Joseph blithely replied, 'Just the supermarket throw-outs, you know, carrots, onions, sometimes a bit of cheese and, needless to say, the odd clove of garlic, but sometimes a few bunches of Grenache or Cabernet Sauvignon, Mourvèdre or even Syrah. I should think Eddie can probably tell you more about what they chuck out at the end of the day. I'm sure that he must have had some experience in his gathering days.'

There was an uncomfortable silence. It was as if the air had stopped and no one was breathing. I realised that Joseph had thrown me a chance to speak as opposed to listen, but there was also discomfort in their faces. Yes, the question was a little out of order but, nonetheless, I took up the gauntlet.

'Yes,' I said as if I was an expert on the subject. 'The best stuff, as I recall, was the Uruguayan cheddar cheese. The supermarkets could never sell it and threw it out at least twice a week. Kept me going for months in the early days, that did … that and the carrots. Strangely, though, it was one of the nicest cheeses I've ever had. D'you know, it had a wonderful underlying hint of garlic, rather akin to Joseph's wine in that respect. It's a shame, though, you can't buy it anywhere now. Someone told me that nowadays the entire production goes off to China.'

There was a ripple of sniggers and Joseph, who was still standing, gave me a gentle pat on the back. 'Here's a toast to Eddie, the Uruguayan cheddar cheese connoisseur, to Ada, and to the highly anticipated prospect of refilling all your glasses with my delicious garlic wine!' Everyone stood and emptied their glasses. For me, it was a moment of acute embarrassment, but Ada didn't seem bothered at all.

The evening passed in much the same way with a little banter and quite a lot of humour until Diana said that she and Dick needed to retire. Joseph had readied their room sometime earlier, and both Ada and I were a little surprised.

'Are you two a couple? Dick, you never told me! So this is all part of a much bigger story! I'm really surprised that I hadn't figured it out. I must be getting rusty.'

Dick responded, 'Ada, it's only by chance that you and Eddie became involved in this. Diana, Joseph, and Oscar have been involved in this business for some time now. Diana and I became very close a while back. So there you are.'

Tom piped up, 'Looks like I'm the new kid on the block in these matters. As you know, I've worked with Dick and Joseph in the past, but never on a game plan like this. I hope to be of some use and learn from you at the same time.'

Well, Tom,' Dick said, 'welcome to the insider's club. Pay attention, keep your nose clean, and avoid garlic breath. It's a dead giveaway. Anyhow, bedtime now! And tomorrow is the start of the final campaign, a gathering of our forces. Rest well, everyone!'

'Tom,' Joseph said, 'you can have the bedroom next to Diana and Dick.'

'Oh dear. Tom, if you snore, please do so quietly,' Dick said.

'Don't worry. I'll play the telly loud enough so you won't hear me.'

Joseph said, 'Dear me, what a motley bunch!' as he followed them, leaving Ada and me to do the washing up.

'Eddie? 'Ada had a serious look on her face. 'What will you do when all this is over?'

'We'll go back to your farmhouse, won't we?'

'No, I don't mean that. I mean, you'll have all this property and land. What will you do with it?'

'I was hoping we could figure that out together. How much would we need to live on and do all the things we want to do? I liked the idea you mentioned of sharing some of it with charities. Honestly, I wouldn't know where to start.'

'It's not so much the houses but the land, Eddie. It's extremely valuable, and because of that, you need to decide what to do with it in case something happens to us. If you leased it to, let's say, Médecins Sans Frontières, that would give them a chance to mine the material themselves, which in turn would ensure that a good charity would benefit from it.

'Let's face it, all those organisations need help, don't they? I should think that the mineral deposits would last only a few years, so you could take the land back when it's all done with and revert it to forestland.

'But there is one other thing, Eddie, which is equally serious. I don't have any close family and you have no family left that we know of. So if anything happened to you, then the state would claim all of your possessions, including any leases you might own and that would be that. If we were to officially unite, then the situation would be different, and I would be able to ensure that your possessions would go to more deserving organisations according to whatever your wishes might be.'

'Are you proposing to me?'

'Well, yes, I suppose I am in a way. But it's only to safeguard your...No, it isn't. It's just an excuse to get my hands on your goods!'

'Oh, that's alright, then.' I laughed and laughed. 'Oh, Ada, you have such a lovely turn of phrase. When shall we do it? The end of next week?'

You can't imagine how that made me feel. She had actually admitted in her own way that we were a little bit more than just companions. It was terrific, something real, something positive in my life. She could see that I was so happy with the suggestion, and as I finished drying the last of the dishes, she put her arms around me and we kissed.

'Bedtime?' she asked. 'Early start tomorrow by the sound of things. We better not be late for breakfast, had we now?'

Chapter 17

For the rest of them, being late for breakfast was to arrive at the table around 8 am. Diana was already finished and was talking at some speed as to what the next step should be in bringing the problem to a head.

'It's Boris Curtain, the county councillor, to start. I have had his bank account checked and it seems that not only has he been receiving considerable amounts of cash but has been transferring it to another account that he opened in Greece. I would assume that when the final deal is done, he will disappear and then reappear in retirement in the care of some eastern European diplomat, and thus we would lose him. So the first thing is to drag him in.

'We'll have to take on the persona of another Soviet gang, something that is on the rise and finding favour within the Russian establishment, as we have all noticed. Then we need to let him go and leave the rest to his present master. It won't be nice nor will it last for too long. They get a bit boisterous when it comes to a beating. So there we have it, number one target dealt with. Once we get confirmation of his demise, then we move on to number two, the Secretary of State.'

It was all a bit frightening. It was like a television spy drama becoming real.

At that moment, a telephone rang. It was Diana's. She listened to the voice very attentively and finally replied with a single word, 'Right.' It's difficult to describe her expression. There was a simmering mirth underlying an outward show of seriousness. When the call ended, she turned to us abruptly.

'It seems that Wragge is dead. The assumption is that he took his own life, having been found this morning at the bottom of Beachy Head. He was obviously thrown over the edge last night, but apparently, he was already dead before that happened. One of our own people was there in the capacity of a forensic analyst and noticed a minute pin prick right at the lower back of his skull, probably the only part of his head that wasn't crushed by the fall. I suppose he was either lethally injected or simply had a needle forced into his brain. I happen to know it's a favourite spot to inject liquid hydrogen just for the fun of it. Well, now we know what we're up against.

'By the way, Richards has now asked for a permanent position in the European division. I think he wants to stay out of the frame for as long as possible and this new status would give him every excuse to keep out of trouble. I've agreed to the request, so that's another one we no longer have to worry about.'

'Who've we got to tackle Boris Curtain?' Dick wondered. 'Who's good at the impersonation of a Russian or eastern European strong-arm? What about Martin?'

Joseph burst out laughing, 'You don't mean Militant Martin, do you? Okay, he's certainly frightening, but Russian ... I don't think he could carry it off.'

Tom asked, 'Have you got any sympathisers in MI6 or the Government Communications Headquarters who speak Russian?'

While everyone racked their brains, Ada returned to the dining room. I was totally out of the discussion. I really had no idea about all this spy stuff. But there they were, three professionals discussing murder.

Ada joined the conversation. 'I don't wish to appear ignorant, but are you talking about doing something illegal?' Her question was met with silence.

Joseph put his hand to his ear. 'Did anybody hear something? I could have sworn that I heard a squeaking noise, didn't you? There must be a mouse in the room!'

Everyone started to laugh, including Ada, but I must say that I thought her question was quite reasonable.

Diana spoke with a more serious tone. 'Ada, my dear friend, we are dealing with dangerous people. The courts can't touch these animals. The only way to get rid of them is to cull them. We would prefer that they got rid of each other, but to do that, it is necessary to feed them some bait. They're usually so greedy that they grab hold of it on the first bite. And that's what we hope will happen now. Militant is a great guy and can be very scary, but the accent will be a problem.'

Diana looked thoughtful, 'I'll tell you what, though. The last evening that I spent with Oscar, he said that Militant had found love with a Polish woman ten years younger than him. I wonder if he's still with her. I hardly think that Curtain could even begin to tell the difference between a Russian and a Polish accent. I know I couldn't.'

Ada turned to me and uttered something that I hadn't the least idea how to translate. After a pause, she started again but in a different accent or language. I couldn't make any sense of it, nor could the others.

Dick laughed. 'Oh my goodness, Ada. I'd forgotten that you and George used to speak a secret constructed language. So I take it that you have just given Eddie directions to the zoo in both Polish and Russian or something like that.'

'Not quite. I told him that we should have Martin and his partner, if she is still with him, round for supper. Eddie and I will do the cooking.' She looked directly at me and said under her breath, 'It will keep you out of sight for an hour or so.'

Joseph agreed and both Dick and Diana nodded their approval. 'Wednesday next week, then? Dick, will you give Martin a ring, or shall I? I think he knows you better.'

Dick thought it was a great idea. I think he admired Militant Martin for being a person who stood up for what was right. As I learned later, he tried to punch a judge once for making what he thought was a wrong decision in a rape case. It involved a friend who was the victim in the case and whom he had known for years. The judge gave Militant thirty days for it, no matter how hard Dick had tried to get him released.

I had never had much to do with Christmas owing to the fact that I never had anyone to share it with. What I found amusing was that, despite all the bright and cheerful decorations hanging up in the streets and on people's houses, our present company focused on disposing of certain individuals. Real spirit of Christmas, I thought, but never mind that. I imagined that those on the other side had no notion of good cheer either.

After the planning talk ended, Ada and Diana had plenty to talk about, and it was good not to hear work mentioned for two whole hours.

***

The following Wednesday was New Year's Eve, and Militant and his companion, Edyta, had been invited to Joseph's celebration dinner. While I washed pans, Ada was putting together a goulash with all sorts of extras, and though I had no idea what they were, it smelled delicious.

I caught snatches of the conversation from the dining room and overheard Militant Martin bringing up certain familiar memories. He mentioned that he had been chucked out of a squat when he was a youngster by the police after running away from 'the home'. I peeped past the door at the speaker and noticed an odd feature that made him unmistakable. He had one narrow, almond-shaped eye, and the other was much more rounded and lacked an eyebrow. I couldn't believe it.

'Soxon, have you got your socks on?' I yelled. You should have seen his face. He jumped up, pulled me out of the kitchen doorway and threw his arms around me.

'My God, Eddie! I never thought I'd ever see you again!' He turned to the others and shouted, 'This is the guy that I ran away with from St Michael!'

How he recognised me, I shall never know. So many years had passed and I'm sure I must have changed quite a bit from young Eddie. Despite that, he recognised me instantly.

Obviously, the conversation turned from the business at hand to memories that he and I shared. He had been bullied and severely beaten by one of the staff at the home, hence the eye defect. It all started with them teasing him about his name, Soxon, which led him to retaliate and the beatings followed. He and I escaped and found an empty house in Southampton that we used as a base, but the police caught him. I managed to get away but that was the last I saw of him, almost forty years ago.

He had been lucky, though, and was rescued by a very good social worker who took him in and gave him a life. But physical scars can become permanent in one's mind, and it seemed that his life was to follow a very rocky path. Nonetheless, when he needed Dick the most, his life changed, and he found a new outlet for his pent-up anger.

'I actually met Dick when he defended me on a case where I was wrongly accused of masterminding a bank heist meant to fund a radical organisation I was loosely allied to. I was involved in security whenever I was needed. Mostly I've worked odd jobs and tried to keep my nose clean though trouble always seems to find me. How about you, Eddie? What have you been up to?'

I told him about my life in a nutshell, though there really wasn't much to tell. I brought him up to date on what was happening with my inheritance, at least as much of it as I understood, and about Ada. 'How did you and Edyta meet?' I asked him.

Martin and Edyta looked at each other and smiled. I detected a slight eastern European accent when she spoke but her English was perfect. 'I'm afraid our meeting was not as exciting as yours and your partner. I was enjoying some drinks at a pub when I noticed this handsome gentleman looking straight at me and smiling. He signalled for me to join him, and I did.'

'I thought she was beautiful...'

Edyta waved him away with a roll of her eyes and continued. 'Anyway, we talked for a few hours and discovered that we were both involved with the same radical organisation and that we both felt strongly about social issues.'

Just then, the kitchen door swung open and Ada appeared carrying a large tureen, and then another and another until the table was completely laden.

'*Smacznego*!' she announced. We all looked at her, startled.

'What's she on about?' someone muttered.

Then Edyta raised her glass. 'She said, "Enjoy!"'

Joseph was already chuckling to himself. 'Come on, you lot. Let's get started!'

I introduced Ada to Edyta and they hit it off straightaway. They sat next to each other and spoke only in Polish, so none of us had any idea what they were talking about. Martin and I continued talking about the old times. Diana and Dick were flirting, leaving poor Joseph and Tom to drink more and more of his superlative garlic-scented wine.

Eventually Joseph stood up and addressed us. 'Much as I hate to disturb your evening merriment, we do have things of a very serious nature to discuss. Dick has already apprised Martin of the situation at hand, and he and Edyta have graciously agreed to help in whatever way they can. Directing himself to them, 'Thank you for supporting our efforts and for joining us tonight. Martin, can you speak with an eastern European or a Russian accent?'

'No, but Edyta can.'

'We know that, but we want you to pretend to be a heavyweight Russian tycoon. Is that something you could pull off?'

'I'm afraid I can't do a credible Russian accent. If I'm not believable, it could put you at greater risk. Any ideas, Edyta?'

'If it's over the phone, it would be easy for me.' Speaking with a very deep and husky Russian accent, she said, 'Good evening. I am calling you to offer you paradise.'

Everyone was startled at how authentic she sounded. 'That's brilliant!' Dick exclaimed.

Diana quickly moved the discussion along. 'Right, that's splendid! We do it over the phone. Here's my plan so far. We'll arrange a rendezvous with Boris Curtain and tip off the other side that he is about to talk to us.

'Tom, can you put together a cryptic message directed to the Secretary of State for the Environment about the meeting with Curtain and make a drop to his office? Have you got a way to do that without being obvious?'

'Yes, I'm sure I can. I'll have to wear a disguise or maybe send a trusted female friend to drop it to his secretary when he's out to lunch. He's very punctual about his lunch breaks. I'll cut and paste a simple message from magazine or newspaper cut-out letters that can't be traced.'

'Excellent! We'll also need to put a script together so that Edyta knows what to say, and we'll take it from there. We'll leave it till after the New Year, give him a chance to enjoy his last one on the planet.'

The last comment was rather doom laden and I think we all felt it. Sensing our disapproval, Diana apologised. 'Sorry about that last thing. It was a bit blunt, I know.'

Joseph, as always, brought life back into the gathering. 'So's this knife!' and as he said it, he pretended to cut his thumb off with the back edge of his table knife. Things soon got back into a festive mood until the clock struck midnight. By that time, the food and drink had well prepared everyone for a good night's rest.

***

We all stayed with Joseph over the New Year and made our final plans. The idea was to offer Boris Curtain a substantial increase in his funding if he would consider joining our so-called enterprise, that being the stealing of my little patch of real estate.

But nothing ever goes as planned, and it immediately fell apart when it came to the dialogue. When Edyta called Boris Curtain a fortnight later, it took less than five minutes for the entire original script to be lost.

'Mr Curtain, my name is Alexei Karaminov. I believe you have a connection in the government of your country regarding the takeover of a patch of land near the city of Southampton. I am willing to double your retainer fee in return for your input to my own plan.'

There was a short silence followed by, 'I'm sorry. There's nothing I can do. The bastard's blackmailing me. If I swap sides now, he'll publish everything he's got on me.'

This was not the expected response, and it threw Edyta off. 'What do I say now?' she whispered with her hand over the phone's mouthpiece.

Joseph stepped forward and took the phone from Edyta. We all looked at each other with alarm wondering how Joseph was going to handle this unexpected reaction from Boris.

'Boris, old chap. You don't know who I am and never will, but as I see it, you don't have any options. You will meet our party at three o'clock tomorrow at the Cornwall Tavern by the ferry port.

'We are fully aware of your involvement in this web of corruption and what the Secretary of State holds on you regarding your past. We, however, are in a position to terminate you and the Secretary of State at any time we wish should you not fully comply. The Secretary is under investigation and will be dealt with accordingly, regardless of his threats to you.

'We do not take no for an answer, and we expect you to arrive without escort or surveillance. Do not even try to make any contact with the Secretary or his minions between now and our meeting. You are under complete observation. Your every move is known, even the colour of your lavatory paper is known, so don't let us down. Because of our interest in you, you are for the moment safe, but you have no escape from us. Three o'clock tomorrow then. Don't forget and do not be late.'

Joseph put the receiver down and took a deep sigh. 'Well, it's done! See what happens now. Who's up for it tomorrow?'

There was the kind of silence that sometimes follows the detonation of a bomb. Diana put her hand up, followed in turn by everyone else. Obviously, there were too many volunteers for the actual meeting, but it did give us the chance to work out the surveillance.

Joseph smiled, somewhat bemused. 'I'm going to give Merry a ring. She'll love all this.'

It was at this point that I began to wonder what my brother Ernest had got us into. Why was this bunch of mad people so keen on stopping the Secretary of State for the Environment from getting his own way, I asked myself. Was there something I missed or didn't know about?

Ada had her odd ways, but this lot, who had seemed so reasonable at the beginning, were now looking like a gang of mobsters who would stop at nothing to achieve their own goals. Dick was probably the sanest, so I decided to ask him quietly out of earshot of the others what they intended to do with the Secretary of State and his people when they finally had them trapped.

'Eddie, you're aware that your little piece of land is worth a great deal of money to certain people. The wealth that will be created will not be used in any ethical way if that particular Secretary of State has any say in it. He was selected for the job of Environment Secretary because of his attitude to the environment, that being if you can't use it for gain or pleasure then concrete it over.

'Take the badger business, for example. It has been scientifically proven that eradicating badgers will have no effect on TB in cattle. But once the badgers no longer exist, planning regulations regarding building on sites where badger setts are known to exist will no longer stop a development. Not only that, but their extermination also throws the whole idea of the badger being a protected species straight out the window. And that's just one example.

'It's just a money game played by the wealthy for the wealthy at the expense of our environment and wildlife and its citizens. What will we do with him? Simple. He will be eradicated just like the badgers unless he decides to resign and take a permanent holiday in Uzbekistan. He needs to feel insecure first, so if we remove all those he is blackmailing, he will lose a great deal of his leverage. It would be as if his trousers were stolen while he was sitting on a public lavatory.'

Quite seriously, it explained further what Ada had told me but I hardly had a clue as to why they were so intent on doing it. Dick looked at me. He could see that what he had said wasn't really enough.

'Eddie, look at it this way. He is a very evil man. He wants to steal something, as it happens, from you. We don't tolerate that kind of behaviour from anyone, least of all from anyone in the government. So, we react.

'Just so you know, we are not funded by the government or any of its agencies but through an international organisation that attempts to neutralise the corruption promoted by powerful people in the public view. There are thousands of such ruthless people and we are but a few. It is a deadly path.

'Look at what happened to Oscar. He was a really special operator who will be very hard to replace. It was my fault in not thinking clearly and inviting him to my club to meet you and Ada. How I regret that.' Despite Diana's assurances, Dick still blamed himself.

He turned and left the room. This whole thing was so much bigger than I had ever imagined. I was uneasy about having the grit to be part of it. But to quit would lose me the one thing that I now treasured ... Ada. I could see in her face the excitement that the whole thing was giving her.

I poured myself a glass of wine and plopped down on a kitchen chair. *Come on, Eddie! Buck up!* I thought to myself. *Tomorrow! Think about tomorrow!* my mind replied.

Chapter 18

Much as Ada wanted to be in the front line, it was generally agreed that it would be best if she and I took a back seat as knowledge of our whereabouts by the other side could compromise any further activity. The target, Mr Curtain, arrived on time in what may be described as a state of total terror. The whites of his eyes were red and raw as if he had been crying for some hours. His clothes were untidy, and one got the impression that what he really longed to do was to tear everything off and jump into a bath of prussic acid. It was sad, really, to see somebody who, for the sake of keeping some kind of misdemeanour out of the public eye, had become totally deranged. It was obvious to Ada and me that the man was alone, both in mind and body, as we watched him from our vantage point in a secluded alcove at the back of the tavern.

Tom casually walked to a bar stool within earshot of Curtain's table. Joseph walked past Boris a couple of times, to the bar and back, checking that there was no other company. He sat down some distance from Boris and pulled out his mobile phone. Within a few seconds, Boris Curtain's phone buzzed and the poor man, with terror on his face, answered the call.

'Mr Curtain, you are on time. Congratulations. Is that usual for you or do you normally like to keep people waiting?' Boris stammered something that we couldn't quite catch. It was enough for Joseph to continue.

'Mr Curtain, go to the window and tell me who is in the blue Ford in the car park.' Boris rose and followed his instruction.

'I don't know. It's a woman. Oh God, I think she's pointing a gun at me!'

'How does that make you feel, Mr Curtain? Go back to your seat and sit down. It is time for us to talk.' Boris Curtain did as he was told. It was obvious that he was terrified.

Merry, who was sitting in the blue Ford, had been holding a small telescope to her eye when he had seen her. He was bound to think the worst. It is in the nature of fear. In the meantime, Militant walked into the tavern, ordered two espresso coffees, and sat down opposite Boris. Militant didn't need to act or pretend to look mean. It was something he could not disguise. Maybe it was the scars across his cheek forming the letter H or perhaps the missing left eyebrow. 'Alright, mate? You look a bit on edge,' Militant said as he placed a cup before Boris.

'Wouldn't you be?' he responded.

'Yes, I suppose I would be under the circumstances. You got a family, Boris?'

Curtain looked at Militant as if he had just read him a death sentence. Boris began to whimper. 'I've got a wife and two little girls. Please don't involve them. They've got nothing to do with this.'

Just then Dick arrived, went to the bar, ordered a cup of coffee, and sat down next to Boris. Ada and I giggled when Dick cheerfully said, 'Well, this is cosy, isn't it?'

Tom remained at his bar stool as a lookout.

Diana was next. She gave Dick a kiss and drew up a chair from another table. 'Hello, darling,' she muttered. 'Oh, is this the famous Mr Curtain? We've heard so much about you. Tut, tut, Mr Curtain. Have you been a naughty boy peeing in the big boys' pool? Not wise, you know. But of course you have! That's why you're here now.'

She took from her pocket a ball bearing and rolled it across the table to him. 'Do you recognise this, Mr Curtain?'

'It's a ball bearing, isn't it?' Boris replied in a frightened, puzzled sort of way.

'Clever man!' Diana retorted, 'But what is it made of? Now that's a good question, isn't it?'

Boris almost choked out his single word reply. 'Rhodium?'

'Spot on, Mr Curtain! Full marks. Now where do you think this has come from? Russia, Whitehall, or somewhere much closer to home?'

I could see that Boris, given a gun at that point, would have probably shot himself. Instead, he completely broke down with tears trickling down into the coffee that Militant had set before him.

Diana continued. 'What can you tell us, Mr Curtain? How much pressure are you under to have allowed yourself to get into this state? What do you know about our good friend Blatherley, you know, the Secretary of State for the Environment? He's a dead man, you know, and I'm sure you don't want to go down with him.

'Now think. If you play along with us then your secret past life will never come to light. However, if you don't, then Blatherley will tell all, not only to implicate you but he will accuse you of masterminding and organising the fraud and will claim that he had ordered an investigation into your activities. So are you in or are you out? Your call.'

Curtain raised his head. There was a pleading look in his eyes, his brow deeply furrowed. 'It was his niece. I didn't know. She and I were just hanging about together. We were only fifteen and then we got kind of serious. He found out two years ago and said that I was up for historic rape if I didn't do what he said. Christ, we were still only kids when it happened, and we did it together. It was not like I forced her. We were really quite serious about each other. Her parents arranged for her to have an abortion and forbade her to ever see me again. Then she killed herself, left me a note saying that she loved me and couldn't suffer being separated from me.

'That bastard Blatherley made out that it was all my fault, and if I didn't do everything that he demanded, he would make sure that I would spend the rest of my life in jail. I'm so screwed up with this. I just want to give up and die. Look, my wife left me ten days ago because she somehow found out that I had a relationship with Anne, Blatherley's niece. But she thought it was like yesterday, not thirty-five years ago. Oh, Christ ... tell me, what can I do?'

'So I take it that the answer to my question is a yes?'

'I'll do anything. Look, I've been involved in so many corrupt deals because of Blatherley, I'd just like to make some kind of amends. To start with, the rhodium business belonged to a chap from Australia. Blatherley got some bent copper from Sussex to bump him off without realising that the man had a niece living in Portsmouth and working in this area. So what does he do? He has her killed too.

'What he wanted me to do was push the probate on the property through without delay, but what with the murders, it was totally impossible. Things just don't work like that, but because he was so used to pushing people around, he thought that I could arrange everything to his advantage. So I've been hedging, trying to buy time. But he's such a bastard, he even had some Russian heavies visit me. I was terrified.

'The thing is, I can't move anything until all the investigations and legal stuff are sorted out by the Court of Probate and that's going to take months what with all the searches that will have to be made. I take it you really want me to change sides and do the same work for you?'

'No, Boris,' Diana growled. 'We are not in the business of gaining trust for political gain. We wish only to see that the fraud ceases to exist. Didn't you know that there's another heir to that estate?'

Boris looked puzzled. 'I'd heard a rumour, but I was told to ignore it because steps were being taken. I assumed that it meant that if a rightful owner did exist, they wouldn't live long enough to enjoy the inheritance.'

'Well, he exists and he is certainly not going to die, but I'll tell you who is ... Blatherley and anyone else who tries to twist the truth in this little saga. We don't care for trials. When the evidence is so strong, we react with alacrity. He will not know anything until we take him, you understand?

'Carry on as you have been with Blatherley. Remember, you are being watched, day and night. We will call you when we are ready, and you must give us any information that you glean from your meeting with the big boss. Understood? Your fate is in your own hands now. Don't lose your grip or you will find that your time here is limited. Do I make myself clear?'

Boris nodded. Joseph stood up, slapped the man on the back and offered him a drink. The bloke looked parched. 'Brandy, old chap? Look, it's just about lunch time. Go and speak to the nice lady in the blue Ford. She's always ready for a meal.'

It was at that moment that Joseph's phone rang. It was Merry.

'Gunmen in black Lexus! Two plus the driver. Do you want me to ram them?'

Joseph didn't hesitate. 'Do it! Put your belt on and duck at the point of contact.'

Merry swung out of her parking place backwards at full throttle. Her tow bar went straight through the rear off-side door of the Lexus. There was a sharp cry from within the Lexus. Someone definitely got hurt.

Ada laughed. 'Flashy Japanese motors. For the money, one would have at least expected armour plating!'

Merry slapped her old Ford into first gear and roared off across the car park in a cloud of blue smoke, taking with her the Lexus door still clinging to her tow bar. One of the gunmen lurched out of the stricken vehicle, raised his gun, and fired three bullets into the rear of Merry's car. Merry crashed into a bollard, her car coming to a standstill. We all held our breaths. The gunman ran up to the driver's door, and as he raised his weapon to fire again, a single shot rang out. Joseph quickly holstered his gun inside his jacket.

'Help me out of here!' came the angry voice from within the Ford. 'That bastard tried to kill me, cheeky bugger!' Merry struggled out of her seat, threw her shotgun on to the back seat, turned, and gave the corpse of the gunman a hefty kick in the ribs.

'Bloody good thing I brought that with me.' She stood there for a minute brushing herself off. 'God, the smoke in there! It's enough to choke you to death. What do they put in those cartridges? Oh, look at my car! What a bloomin' mess!'

Joseph was already on his phone, and shortly after, a white van and a tow truck arrived at the scene.

Merry was livid. 'Did you see that? The cheeky monkey! If that's all they've got on their minds, to bump an old lady off, then the world is in a very sorry state. Just look at her! I liked that old Ford, but now she's all banged up!'

Dick put his arm around her. 'Don't worry, Merry. We'll get it fixed up just as it was unless you'd like a new one. Besides that, you look really lovely even though you still have gun smoke rising out of your hair. It's very becoming, by the way.'

'I wouldn't want another one of those. They're nothing but bloomin' trouble! And don't be so bloody personal about my appearance. That's not gun smoke. It's my brain boiling! Can't you tell the difference?'

It was a conversation of impossibilities and was eventually passed over as Joseph gave funerary directions for the Lexus. Its wounded occupant, being unable to walk or run, quickly succumbed to Joseph's thumb and forefinger judiciously applied to the base of his neck. Of the driver, there was no sign, his exit having been achieved within seconds of the collision.

The car park was entirely cleared of broken glass and debris within ten minutes. Boris looked completely cowed by what he had seen, if not a little impressed.

'I believe you understand now who we are, and I'm sure that you don't want to join the legions of those missing without a trace, do you now, Boris?' Diana could really be threatening when she felt it was necessary. 'Now off you go. We'll contact you soon. Remember, there are no options for you in this business. Do as we say or you will suffer the same as those two. Clear?'

Boris took the hint and scurried away to his car. His walk was that of a man trying not to run, but he gave in at the last twenty yards. Even that was a struggle as he tripped and fell at the last hurdle over a raised stone in the tarmac. He lay there for a while before lifting his head and pushing himself up. We looked on, almost feeling sorry for him, as he opened his car and sat for several minutes without moving. Eventually he started the engine and slowly drove away.

Diana stood watching with Joseph. 'Do you think he'll be reliable?'

'It depends on how soon we can nail Blatherley. I think if we can deal with him then Boris might survive long enough to take his pension. I think he has been weak and allowed himself to be led down that path. Let's face it, Blatherley had nothing on him that would have any value in a court.'

Merry sidled up to Joseph. 'Come on, hand them over!'

'Hand what over?'

'The hardware ... as if you didn't know. Remember, I'm the armourer now, and I'm the one who makes sure that everything is oiled up and ready should it be necessary, and it will be very soon. We all know that, don't we? By the way, what the hell is all this about? I like it, whatever it is, but no one has told me anything. Who was that guy? He looked really upset.'

'Merry, I'll explain everything a little later, but first, I want you to do something for us, besides being Captain Pugwash. We need to have a gathering of the gang, that's everybody in the group including your cat, okay? Diana has to go back to

Yorkshire next week and we need to discuss with everyone what strategy we should follow. I suggest that we go to Charleston Manor and then on to the tea rooms at Wilmington for lunch. I know it's some distance, but I'll pick up the tab for the fuel and food. Diana leaves on Wednesday, so let's try for Monday. Is that agreeable?'

Merry pondered for a moment. 'I'll see what I can do.'

'Okay, everyone. Let's get out of here before the police arrive.'

Chapter 19

The Secretary of State immediately recognised the number on his mobile. Under his breath, he said, 'Poor timing. I'm in a meeting right now. Can this wait?'

'I'm afraid not,' Basilisk said. 'Can you get away?'

The Secretary let out an exasperated sigh, disconnected the call, and announced, 'Gentlemen, I'm afraid I must cut the meeting short. An emergency has come up. Let's set up a follow-up meeting for Thursday at one o'clock. Is that agreeable to everyone?'

A shuffle of papers and mobile calendars was followed by a general consensus. 'Splendid! Have a good afternoon, gentlemen.'

He rushed off to his office and addressed his secretary. 'Greta, hold all my calls for now, please.'

'Yes, sir. Oh, by the way, someone dropped off this envelope addressed to you. I'm afraid I don't know when it was left here, but I found it partly slipped under my blotter this morning.'

'Thank you,' he mumbled as he picked up the envelope by a corner and dashed into his office, locking the door behind him. Donning latex gloves, he cautiously unsealed it with a sharp letter opener. On the single page were cut-out letters spelling, 'BC meeting with Sphinx. 16-1:1500 Cornwall Tavern.'

'That bastard!' He picked up his mobile and dialled.

'Basilisk.'

'Where are you?' enquired the Secretary of State.

'Somewhere safe. You should know better than to ask.'

'I just received a strange note without a sender's ID. Was that you?'

'Perhaps, but you should've received it days ago. I need to have a word with my pigeon. Anyway, I took care of it ... sort of.'

'What's going on?' asked the Secretary impatiently.

'I'm well-entrenched inside Sphinx. Adam and Eve have amassed several cronies looking after their interests and they're getting dangerously pushy and antsy. They know who the wizard is behind the curtain. Seems like they're trying to get to you through your weakest links. The attempt on JP failed, and your hit contractors, whom I invited to the meeting between BC and Sphinx, failed miserably. Some old biddy rammed them with her car and badly injured a passenger. One was shot dead and the third scurried off like a rat fleeing a feral cat. We need to do better than that.

'You should know that they're well-armed, thanks to the old lady and Eve's cache. Still don't know where she keeps it.'

'First things first,' said the Secretary of State. 'I should've gotten rid of the canary a long time ago. At some point, we need to find out where Eve keeps her cache and destroy it. The ultimate goal is to destroy Sphinx. I understand they're sitting ducks at JP's mansion. I've got an idea on how to get MI6 involved in eliminating the lot with false information. It'll be like shooting fish in a barrel. Meanwhile, stay clean and focused. There will be a huge reward for you when we pull this off. I'll give you a call when everything's arranged.'

Chapter 20

Right after the tavern incident, we all gathered at a pub a few blocks away for drinks and a quick bite to eat. We were seated at two adjoining tables, and as the groups chatted, my mind drifted as it so often does.

It was funny to think that a year ago, I had not thought of ever becoming part of a group let alone being emotionally connected to anyone like Ada. She definitely fit in better with the rest of them than I did and knew very well that there were times when I struggled with things. But she was patient enough to explain stuff I didn't quite understand when we were on our own.

I was really glad to have met up with Militant again, though. He'd not changed a great deal in the way that he saw things, and that made me feel a little more comfortable when the group came together. I followed his lead in a way. He was much more settled than I was.

Despite all the excitement, I'd be glad when it was all over and Ada and I could go home and live in peace. Being in this situation was like being caught up in a whirlwind, what with Joseph calmly bumping off the gunman outside the tavern without even looking back.

It still made me wonder what sort of guy he was. He was so focused and seemed to see everything in black and white, or so it appeared. Even his walk was direct. He never altered course. When something needed to be done, he did it, and when it was over, it was immediately forgotten because there was always something else that needed to be done. It seems a little complicated but that's how it appeared to me.

I was absolutely fed up with being Mr Grantham. I didn't feel like a Grantham and I was sure that Ada didn't either. I thought we needed to have a chat with Dick and Joseph about it. I knew there was still quite a lot of danger out there, but I was sure that the opposition knew quite well that I existed and that Ada and I were together.

Coming out of my thoughts, I could see Ada and Merry chatting at the other table and I thought I might join them. Militant and Edyta had slipped away and Dick, Joseph, Tom, and Diana were in a serious conversation that I really didn't feel like being a part of.

'Can I join you two?' I asked Ada.

'Merry has just given me a present for the two of us, haven't you, Merry?'

'Yes, something that I think you're going to need very, very soon.'

I was puzzled, but not for long. Ada opened her bag and I could see the barrels of two 9 mm Mausers pointing up at me.

'They're a bit more powerful than your little pea shooters. Oh, and I nearly forgot. I raked these out of the boot before the cleaners took the Lexus away. I think there must be at least thirty to forty rounds in there. Here are a couple of spare clips should you need them.'

She quickly popped the box of bullets and clips into Ada's bag. 'Thanks, Merry. Eddie, carry my bag, will you? It's getting a bit weighty. Merry, was there anything else in the Lexus that might come in useful?'

'Why, yes, come to think of it. There was a map of the Isle of Wight with Joseph's house marked with a circle. That's really why I've given those guns to you. When those two guys don't return, there will be some trouble ... big trouble. You haven't seen the defences at Joseph's yet, have you? The place is like a fortress, and provided his early warning system works properly, there will be a lot of blood on his lawn.'

You know, listening to Merry was almost intimidating There she was, a five-foot-three, plump fifty-five-year-old behaving like a mad dog. I just hoped that the rest of the gang was as motivated as she was because, like she said, there was trouble on its way.

It was true. Joseph's house was like a fortress, the original building designed primarily to ward off invaders. The ground floor dated back to the thirteenth century with walls almost a yard thick. Those old remnants had two storeys above ground level, probably added in the seventeen or eighteen hundreds. The original ground floor was built over a cellar which contained Joseph's wine racks and a central well that was fed by an underground spring. There were also a couple of alcoves fitted with grills, which were obviously intended for captives. The whole had been cut from sandstone, leaving adze marks where the material had been chiselled away. There was a door which opened into a long chamber extending beyond the perimeter of the building which, I was soon to learn, was used as a firing range.

Personally, I thought that the cellar was quite cosy and warm, but that notion was not really shared by any of the others, except perhaps the neighbour's cat. To ensure that intruders were held at bay, the whole building was surrounded by a narrow brook not unlike a small millrace with the main door reached by a stone bridge. The cat flap at the back of the house was accessed from the garden by a fallen tree. Altogether, with all the antique furnishings, velvet curtains and oriental rugs covering the stone walls, it definitely carried the past into the present, and once inside, the cold winter air seemed far, far away.

Chapter 21

When we got back to the house, Ada and I became worried. Joseph hadn't returned and the lights were all out. It was already dark and we weren't quite sure of the pathway to the main door. Ada waved her arms trying to activate the lights that led the way, but they wouldn't come on.

'What do you think, Ada?' I whispered.

'Not sure, but give me one of those pistols, take yours and leave the bag in the hedge here. We need to get off this pathway at once.'

As we turned, we heard a distinct thud as something struck a tree trunk on our left. Then came the whisper, 'Here, quick, keep your heads down.' We did just that and followed the voice.

'Militant, what are you doing here?'

'Trying to stay alive! Joseph's gone round the back with Edyta and Merry. Diana and Tom went round the other way, and I saw Dick walk straight ahead into the bushes. We can't work out where the shooters are hiding. There's no way that they can be inside, not with Joseph's security. So where the hell are they? It doesn't help that whoever is out there is probably using a silencer.'

I suddenly noticed that Ada was no longer with us. 'Where the...?'

Three shots rang out, then silence. We could hear the sound of footsteps running then another two shots. This was followed by some automatic pistol fire, and then nothing.

'Militant, where are you?' It was so dark that I couldn't see him lying on the ground until I trod on him.

'You've found me!' he groaned. 'I think I lost a finger in that last barrage. Have you got a handkerchief or something to stop the bleeding?'

Sure enough, he was missing his left little finger.

'Oh shit, I won't be able to whistle "Sonny Boy" anymore!'

I wasn't sure what he was talking about, but I admired his apparent lack of concern. But where was Ada? That was my main worry.

I would have thought that the amount of time I had spent in the wild would have sharpened my night vision but it was one of those pitch-black nights. I thought I'd better do something to find her. At that moment, I heard the sound of something being hauled nearby. For an instant, as the moon glinted from between the clouds, I saw someone dragging what appeared to be a body out between the hedges. I called out, 'Ada, is that you?'

'Yes, keep your head down and get over here by this wall!'

I made a dash towards her voice and fell forward when I tripped on the stonework. It was just as well that I did. As I fell, another shot rang out, and the bullet caught the heel of my shoe and took it clean away. 'Bloody hell! That was a bit close, wasn't it?'

'Sod that, Eddie! Dick's been shot. Help me drag him towards that hedge where he can't be seen.'

We pulled Dick by his legs, still conscious and in obvious pain. 'Sorry, Dick. Let me take a quick look.' Ada shone her small torch on his torso, where blood could be seen seeping from his chest. 'Dick, I need to find Joseph so he can call for help. I know you're in pain, but try to hang in there. Will you do that?'

Dick nodded. 'Go,' he whispered. 'I'll be okay. Find Diana.'

'Ada, where do you think the others are? This doesn't seem to be following the plan.'

'Did you dump the bag back there?'

'No, I'm still holding it. Why?'

'Because Merry had tucked something else away in there that I need.'

I handed the bag to her, and after a few seconds of blindly searching inside of it, she pulled out a tube that looked like a dynamite stick. Soon, there was a loud hissing as she flung the flare out into Joseph's garden. It was truly terrifying what happened next.

A barrage of automatic fire came from several directions but fortunately not aimed at us. An eerie silence followed that seemed to last forever. It was finally broken by the whirring of a generator, and at last, there was light.

At first, the lights in the house came on, followed by various lanterns scattered around the garden.

'Everybody alright?' It was Joseph's voice. 'Is that Dick lying over there? What's happened!'

'Dick took one in the chest back there. He's going to need medical assistance as soon as possible,' Ada said as she inspected his wound again.

'Joseph, is Diana with you?' Dick was having a hard time breathing and could hardly get the words out.

'No, I haven't seen her since we left the tavern.'

His answer was alarming. We were suddenly faced with the possibility of another close friend's mortality, something even more harshly felt by Dick.

'I'll see if I can find her, Dick,' Joseph assured him, 'Don't worry. She's a tough woman and she'll know how to handle any threats. Right now, we need to get you some help.'

Militant spoke up. 'I saw Diana go round towards the back of the house with Tom when the group broke up to search for the gunmen. I think I could use some medical assistance myself,' he said as he held up his bloodied hand. 'Got my finger shot off. And where is Edyta? Have any of you seen her?'

'Bugger!' Ada loved to use that word, especially when she didn't like all the possibilities that were presenting themselves at any given moment. 'Bugger! Bugger! Bugger! Where are they? I haven't seen Merry either!'

We were all worried about our missing colleagues, but it was clear that Dick needed treatment quickly. A bullet had entered his upper right chest and he started to cough up a lot of blood.

'Hang in there, Dick. Please hang on!' Ada said as she put pressure on his wound with her hand, making him wince. 'We're getting help.'

Joseph called one of his confidential contacts, a surgeon who moonlighted as a sympathiser and could be counted on for emergencies like this. 'Don is a good friend and will help us, no questions asked. Hospital personnel are required to report gunshot wounds to the police and we can't have that,' he explained.

Militant had found his little finger, but after taking a good look, decided that the shattered bone could not possibly be reattached. I heard him mutter under his breath, 'Bastards! Sorry, Eddie. I'm afraid I've made a mess of your handkerchief.'

I thought it was really sad, having only just met him again after so many years, that he had got involved in what was really part of my problem and had lost his finger in the process. For some reason, he didn't seem too bothered. It made me wonder what other close calls he'd been involved in.

It was a tremendous relief when out of the darkness of the lane appeared three figures.

'What are the roadworks doing along there, Joseph? It looks like your electricity supply has been snipped.' Diana appeared genuinely surprised.

'What the hell's been going on here?' Tom asked, looking around wide-eyed.

'Thank God you're okay! We thought you'd all been killed. Diana, Dick's been shot and needs urgent care. I've already called Don the surgeon to assist us.' Joseph pointed to where Dick was lying. 'Let him know that you're okay, Diana.'

Diana's face revealed the shock she felt but she managed to speak to Dick reassuringly in a calm manner. It must have taken a lot out of her not to fall apart, seeing him in that state.

We all huddled around Dick, offering support out of the line of fire, I hoped. But where were they and how many were there? Who were they?

Almost reading my mind, Joseph said, 'It's anyone's guess who these hitmen are and how many are out there but we can pretty much deduce who wants us out of the way.'

'Well, it's awfully quiet out there,' I said, my voice shaking a little. The sudden silence except for the hoot of an owl in the distance and our hushed voices was making me very uneasy.

'Assuming they haven't gone far and may be regrouping, I think we should move into the house while we wait for the surgeon,' suggested Joseph.

Diana, Joseph, and I carried Dick carefully into the sitting room and gently sat him in an oversized chair. He was getting paler by the minute.

Before long, a small speedboat was heard heading for the jetty below Joseph's garden. Joseph went out to meet the surgeon, carrying a gun by his side.

'Good evening, everyone.' Don dropped his Gladstone bag beside him and got to work examining Dick's wound. 'Right. I'm giving him a little morphine to ease his pain, but I need to get that slug out of his chest and stop the bleeding into his lung. Is anyone here good with this type of surgery? I'm going to need some assistance.'

Edyta immediately volunteered. 'I'm up for it, but we also need to attend to Militant's finger,' she said. Militant had been cussing to himself as the pain gradually increased. 'Don't worry, Martin.' she said. 'You can always grow a new one.'

Militant pretended to be overjoyed. 'Will I really, really grow a new one? How about we plant the old one and see if it grows a new hand, too!'

It was just as I had always remembered him at the orphanage. He was either the clown or the idiot and here he was being both in spite of his pain. I recalled that after he had been beaten up by the staff member and kicked several times in the head, he commented in the most matter-of-fact way, 'That baboon has got really big feet, you know. I hope he gets athlete's foot. That'll teach him!'

'Joseph, would you mind if I used your dining room table as a surgical bed?'

'No problem, Don. What else do you need?'

'Let's get some comforters for a mattress. Also a small table for my instruments and a bright lamp without a shade. Where can I wash my hands?'

Once Don's makeshift operating theatre was in place, we carefully laid Dick on the improvised cushioned table. 'I'll be giving him another shot of morphine to further sedate him. I'm going to ask all of you to please wait outside now.'

We all sat in the foyer outside the closed double doors of the dining room and nervously chatted while waiting for the procedure to end. About an hour later, Don came out and spoke with us. 'I was able to remove the bullet, but his vital signs aren't stable yet as he's lost a lot of blood. I've put in a call to Fran, a trustworthy friend who's a nurse and has connections in our blood bank. She'll be by shortly and will stay with Dick until he's stable. He's still quite drowsy at the moment, so I suggest that he be allowed to quietly rest until the nurse gets here. Now where can I find the gentleman with the wounded finger?'

We sat in the foyer for a while longer in case Dick woke up and needed assistance. Chatting quietly, we discussed the day's events and what our next steps should be.

'I wonder how they knew about the meeting at the tavern and that we'd all be gathered here,' Ada said to no one in particular.

'I suppose they could've followed us here,' Tom said, 'but you're right about how they knew in the first place. Do you suppose Curtain's phone could've been tapped?'

Ada speculated, 'How about your phone, Joseph? Could they have eavesdropped on your conversations?'

'That's possible but unlikely. I only use my mobile, not my landline, to communicate sensitive information. My phone detects and censors any spyware attached to it as do Diana and Dick's mobiles. I should have thought of this before but let me show everyone how you can discover and safeguard against eavesdropping malware.'

Merry said, 'Go slowly, Joseph. My ageing brain cells are already giving me a headache just listening to you.'

I knew exactly how Merry felt. All of this complicated spy stuff and newfangled contraptions were Greek to me and, frankly, of little interest. I'm sure Ada would get it quicker than I could.

Once the lesson was over, Ada and Merry went outside with their weapons drawn to suss out if the assassins were still out there. I must say, I admired Ada's fearlessness but it always worried me no end.

A few minutes later, a hail of gunshots rang out in or near the garden. Voices, some unrecognisable, could be heard yelling warnings mixed with grunts of pain. *My God, Ada's out there!* I rose and rushed to the garden's exit door.

'Eddie, don't go out there!' yelled Joseph as he grabbed my arm. 'Are you trying to get yourself killed?'

'But Ada...'

'Don't worry about her! She and Merry are more than capable, so just wait till the gunfire stops.'

Soon, the gunfire ceased as quickly as it had started. We all ran out to the garden, and through the haze of gun smoke, we were shocked at what we saw.

'Here they are, caught in *flagrante delicto*!' said Merry smugly. Around them lay four bodies, bloodied and in grotesque postures ... dead. I ran to Ada and held her. 'Ada, I was so worried! Are you okay?'

'Oh, Eddie, I'm fine.'

'Do any of you recognise these thugs?' asked Merry.

'Bloody hell! Yes, I do!' said Diana in disbelief. 'That's Jeremy Duckworth from MI6. This is just terrible! Blatherley has come up with some real shit this time. He's a dead man walking, that's for sure.'

'My God!' Merry exclaimed in shock. 'Are you telling me that we just shot the good guys?'

'It looks that way, but how were you to know when they don't appear to have any identifiable insignia? Joseph, I need to make an urgent call. Can I use your study? I can't be overheard in there, can I?'

Joseph agreed but we all knew what Diana had to do, and after a short while, she returned in a mood which was half triumphant and half angry. 'Apparently, Blatherley knew what we are and where we are. I'm not sure how he found out but it's certainly bad news. He told someone in MI6 that we were a quasi-anarchist terrorist group and that we needed to be stopped. He also told them that this place was a bomb-making factory.

'Needless to say, all four of the dead men here are MI6 operatives, one of whom had been at one time embedded within an eastern European human-trafficking gang. So Blatherley has even more blood on his hands now.

'Eddie, that patch of land you've inherited is obviously worth a lot more than any of us imagined. After I gave them the bad news, MI6 told me that they're pulling out immediately and said that it would be good if we could finish the business as soon as possible. The agent made it clear that the incident would be thoroughly investigated as per standard protocol.

There's nothing for anyone to worry about. Just give truthful answers to their questions and we should be alright. So there we are. Anyway, how's Dick? I need to see him.'

Diana had barely left the room before her mobile phone started to ring. 'Answer that, will you, Joseph?'

Surprisingly, it was Richards calling her from Brussels. 'Who am I speaking to? Is Diana Plowright there?' Joseph answered that she was unavailable. Richards carelessly blurted out, 'It's Richards here calling from Brussels. Tell Diana that there is a group of five men from the Crimea who were spotted a little while ago boarding a Russian freighter bound for Southampton. According to our information, the vessel docked a few days ago. From what I can gather, they're part of a private army recruited by some Russian oligarch or other, but we are not sure who. We have been warned that the group is known to be bloody-handed, if you get my meaning.'

'Thanks, Richards. I'll pass the message on. The information is appreciated.' Joseph put the phone back in Diana's bag. He hummed to himself as he walked to his sideboard. 'Anyone for a glass of wine?'

Chapter 22

It was not long before a pizza delivery was made. The only difference was that we weren't having pizza that night. Instead, it was a lifesaver for Dick, who was not doing well at all. Three pints of good red, two litres of saline and four metres of tubing were tucked away in the insulated box that the pizza delivery nurse carried on the front of her bike.

'Good evening. I'm Fran,' she said to no one in particular. 'Can you please bring a tall lamp and a wire coat hanger? Where's the patient?' she asked curtly. Within a few minutes, she had set up Dick's transfusion using the implements she had requested.

'He should start to make some improvement in a few hours. I am here for the night and there will be a replacement arriving at eight tomorrow morning. Can you make this room a bit warmer, please?'

'Sorry about the cold,' Joseph muttered. 'Some idiots have dug up our electrics but I'll light a fire in the grate. It'll take a while to warm up.'

Ada gave me a shove. 'Get moving, Eddie. Find some kindling and some wood. We'll get some snacks sorted out while you're out there. Keep your eyes open. Joseph, what shall we do with those corpses?'

'Ask Eddie to get them into the coach house for the moment. MI6 will have to take them away tomorrow, I hope. It's a shame, it really is. I understand that they were a decent bunch. Oh, by the way, Diana told them to get our electrics fixed as well pronto. I hope they don't make a mess of it. There's a lot of spaghetti down there. God knows how they ever found it. That really surprised me. I think I need to give this setup a lot more thought. I don't want this happening again.' And he was gone.

Tom came along to lend me a hand. We found enough kindling under an old chestnut tree which had more or less come to the end of its life. Fortunately, it had been drying for a while and the wood was easy to get started. There was a pile of logs in the outhouse which we carried in for the fire as well.

Once I'd finished, I got started on the bodies. It's startling how the dead become like lead. Try to lift them and one's likely to really damage the spine. Bearing that in mind, I plopped them one at a time onto Joseph's sack barrow. It's funny how useful those things are. Every household should have one.

There were four of them. Three were around thirty to thirty-five, all apparently quite fit but unfortunately now dead. The fourth was a lot younger, maybe twenty, like Marina, much too young to die. It seemed to me that all those deaths over a stupid piece of land was such a tragedy. All those grieving families, so much loss and sorrow. And for what? Plain, unadulterated greed. I can always easily give that a miss. It's good to be comfortable, but to go to those extremes to fill one's coffers is so disgusting.

In the coach house, I propped up the four in sitting positions. Their heads lolled to one side or the other with their shoulders slumped forward, and there I was looking straight into the chasm. I sat down and just looked at them. There was nothing there, just death. No hope, no afterlife, just empty everlasting nothingness. It was only Ada's voice calling me to eat that broke the saddening thoughts, and I returned to the warmth of my new family.

There was a general feeling of depression as I walked in. Things had broken down. Joseph's confidence seemed to be fading and Diana was downright furious that MI6 had fallen for Blatherley's story. 'Anarchists, bomb factory, and what a bloody response! Heaven help a badger if it ever went to poo in Blatherley's backyard!'

I hadn't thought too much about my brother Ernest or Marina for a while, but now they suddenly entered my mind. She was Ernest's daughter and must have been mortified when he was murdered. And then she was killed. Was there anyone to mourn for her as she must have done for her father? Probably not.

But they were my family, and under a different set of circumstances, I might have got to know them and for them to know something about me. But Blatherley stole that from us, destroyed what could have been in a most horrible way. That was the first time I had actually started to hate somebody and realised that it was time for me to play a greater part in all that was going on. I was just beginning to wake up.

'Ada, can we have some target practice tomorrow? I need to make sure that I will be of some use when the time comes. I've been asleep for too long.'

Joseph smiled. 'Diana will take you both downstairs to the range in the morning. We'll have to return the weapons that MI6 was using. But you can still use the Mausers if you like.'

Ada rose. 'Back in a tick!' she said and disappeared upstairs to our room.

God knows where she got them from or where she had hidden them but it would have been funny had they not looked so striking. She laid them out on the table and slowly, carefully loaded the chambers. I had never seen pistols like them before, but there they were, a perfect pair sitting on the kitchen table next to a tureen of cauliflower remnants.

Even Joseph was staggered. 'Where the hell did you get those?'

'I packed them with the rest of our luggage. Left my winter warmers back on the moors and popped these in instead. Eddie had the ammo in what he thinks is his collection of dog collars.'

Everyone looked at me bewildered. Yes, I did have a collection of dog collars. Whenever I found a dead dog by the side of the road, I used to take its collar just in case I met the owner so that I could return it as a memento. But I never met any of the owners, so the collars just grew in number. I had them in a Tesco bag for a while but the handles eventually gave way. I hid them in a hollow tree until I found a hold-all.

I looked at the faces gathered around the table and the expressions were priceless, but how could I not admit the truth. I was coming to the realisation that what I was becoming and what my life had been was too bizarre for some people, especially males, to accept and understand. Many lacked sympathy for what might be thought of as a failing. I looked at Ada, questioningly.

She said, 'Well, I had to say something about the guns, didn't I? So I told the truth.'

'Ada, do you mean to say that I've been carrying ammunition around for the last couple of months without realising it?'

'In a word, yes.'

'How many rounds?'

'Ooh, about two hundred.'

'No wonder it was so heavy!'

By this time, Merry, who had been giggling uncontrollably, had to go to the loo. Joseph choked on his wine. Diana was kind of po-faced; she obviously thought that I was totally out of my mind. Militant and Edyta were almost on the floor, and Tom looked bewildered. Fortunately for me, the evening was saved by the appearance of Fran, Dick's nurse.

'He's hungry. Is there anything that he can have? Me, too, for that matter.'

'There are a couple of warmed pasties in the oven. Help yourself to juice or whatever you like from the fridge. I'm sure Joseph won't mind. Is Dick strong enough to join us?' inquired Diana.

'Not just yet, perhaps tomorrow as long as he rests well. It's a nasty wound and one thing he doesn't need is laughter, so you lot carry on. Right now he's resting comfortably in a chair. I'll stay with him and eat there.'

The mood in the room had changed with thoughts of Dick. It had been a close call for him and I know Ada was a little uneasy about what was going on. So far, we had done well, but after what Richards had said, none of us was really safe.

'Diana,' I asked, 'what is your connection with MI6. You have a lot of sway with the director. How come he failed to realise that you were involved in this business?'

It was the right time and the right question. Even Joseph acknowledged it. We needed allies, not enemies.

'Right,' she replied, 'this is our situation, as Joseph has explained. My cover is that I am working as a police officer. However, we are totally outside government control and we need to be because it is the government we are watching most of the time. We are respected in that we dispose of corruption in high places, whether the government of the day likes it or not. We are funded internationally, not by financiers but by a secret organisation that tries to clean up some of the bad elements in the world, albeit in a small way but nonetheless in an effective way.

'There are similar groups all over the world, each one trying to achieve the same ends, basically to do away with corruption by those in power. Blatherley is a prime example. You have seen the lengths to which he has gone in order to achieve his aims. It is for us to stop him any way we can by doing whatever it takes. Now and then, I call on MI6 to brief the director as to what we are doing and to find out whether there is any counterplot underway against us or if any of our intelligence has been comipted.

'This time something went desperately wrong. Blatherley got past the director somehow and was ordering the troops himself. Bad news for the troops and for the director. That's basically it. By the way, we will all be paid at the end of this, not a lot but enough to cover food and expenses, ammo, etc.' With a short laugh, she said, 'That's if we live long enough!'

'Everything comes out of expenses, even our coffins!' Merry said as she settled down next to Edyta. 'Glad you came, luv?' Merry asked her. Edyta gave her a glum look and uttered something in Polish which sounded a little grim.

All the time that Diana spoke, I was thinking about Ada's secrecy. When did she decide to switch my dog collars for the ammunition pistols, and where had she been keeping it before that? I thought I would ask her a little later when we were alone. It wasn't a question of trust – don't get me wrong – but one of curiosity. She was and is just about as crazy as Merry but in a different way, and she was also the woman that I was hoping to live with for the foreseeable future. I had always felt safe around her, even if she had got a pair of what looked like Colt-duelling pistols.

Coming out of my deep thoughts, I noticed that Joseph was looking at me with a half- smile. 'Don't worry, Eddie, she did the switch back in York, at Dick's sister's place. Then Dick sent the rest of your stuff to me after you moved in. Let's face it, Eddie. What good could you achieve with – how many is it – fifty-seven dog collars?'

I was rather surprised that he had read my mind but I was determined not to let him get away with it. 'Well, how many of the others are now eating dirt? About nine, isn't it? That means all we need to do is get another forty-eight of the buggers and they could all wear a dog collar each.'

'Now that's an idea, Eddie. But on the contrary, if we can recruit fifty-seven acolytes including ourselves, we could all have one each, couldn't we?'

I had no idea what acolytes were so I decided to just drop the conversation. But I could see that the subject was not going away when Militant jumped up and proclaimed, 'Nobody puts a dog collar on me! I'm an atheist!' Then when Merry said she would look good in a diamante one, I knew that the whole thing had become total nonsense.

***

All was quiet for a while, giving us a chance to recover and regroup. Dick was out of danger and recovering. It was on the third night as we all sat in the sitting room planning for the next attack that we heard a cat miaowing.

Joseph jumped up and went to the side window where he thought the sound came from. Quickly turning to us, he shouted, 'To arms, they've arrived! So far, there is one to the left of the coach house. Listen out for the other calls. Lights out, everybody. Someone tell Fran to get Dick out of sight if she can. Under the bed if necessary. There may be some bullets flying about.'

Ada and I took our positions at a first-floor window behind a heavy metal screen. Joseph was fully prepared for this sort of thing and directed the situation with total precision. There were no further warnings, so we assumed that this was no more than for reconnaissance. Not a shot was fired, but Joseph tracked every step the intruder made with the help of security cameras and sensors which picked up movement on a computerised grid map.

It was around 11.30 pm and pitch-black outside without the moonlight except for various areas highlighted by the grounds' lanterns and motion-sensing flood lights. The generators had already started to run deep in the cellar and were inaudible but for a very low rumble. This time there was no chance of a systems failure.

Ada had seen the man, and I could see her finger gradually tightening on the trigger. She followed him in the sights of the pistol as he darted from cover to cover.

'Ada, no! Not now! Wait for Joseph to give the word.' But it was too late. The man dropped like a stone. She had fired only two quick rounds and I think the victim had caught both of them. I must say it takes some doing to shoot a pistol like that, but she seemed to know precisely how to do it.

Everyone drew their weapons and took positions near windows except for Tom who stood by the front door. It was just as well because within a few minutes there was a sharp burst of automatic fire which smashed some of the downstairs windows. Joseph called out, 'Five of them! One on your left, Militant! Merry, look to the left of the statue of Minerva! Ada, coach house door, two!'

It was like a war zone. Militant, being left-handed, was having trouble firing his weapon with his right and wasn't doing too well. He must've missed hitting his target miserably as every time he fired a shot, he'd groan, 'Dammit! Missed!' and then he'd go through the same procedure again after the next shot. Merry, on the other hand, was like a proper trooper and was only slowed down by having to reload. Ada was her normal self, as cool as she could be.

'These are such nice weapons,' she said as if talking to herself. 'They're just the right weight.'

My job was to reload the chambers as she methodically emptied one pistol after the other. Seeing revolvers like that, floral-engraved Buntline Specials with eleven-inch barrels, I was beginning to understand the love affair with the gun. Awful to think about it now, but it was there, real and cold-blooded.

'You know, Eddie, one thing about my grandfather. He really knew about guns!' Ada would say.

She was an excellent shot, and still is. Two of the targets fell almost as soon as she opened fire. I could hear Merry chuckling as she blasted away without much care as to what or whom she was shooting. Joseph was more accurate. Even Militant scored a hit which made the assailant scream with pain. 'Gotcha!' he murmured triumphantly.

Joseph yelled for silence, and we waited for a full ten minutes before he declared that the present danger was over. The only sound was that of Militant's victim wailing.

There was another miaow and we all took cover except for Joseph, who went to the kitchen door and pushed the cat flap open. 'Come on, Dippy! Have you come for your lentils?' Dippy was a neighbour's cat who had discovered that Joseph had a predilection for tinned lentils and always expected her bowl to be full whenever his was filled. 'They might be cheap, but it's the expectation that gets you in the end. At least she doesn't mind them cold.'

'Come on,' he instructed. 'Let's bring that idiot who's groaning out there inside. Check the others to make sure they're actually dead and shove them into the coach house. It's like a bloody mortuary in there already but without the refrigeration. God, I hope they get rid of the lot tomorrow.'

'I don't know whose running that bunch anymore. It used to be their own commanders, then one day another lot turned up, said they were from MI5. Shortly after, some more in a green and red van arrived and claimed to be the environmental health. I never did find out who sent them.

'Anyway, grab all the weapons and any extra ammunition and go through their pockets. I want as much information as I can get to assess the size and numbers that may end their days in my garden. This is not over by a long shot. Blatherley's fellow conspirator will send everything he's got when the news of this failure gets back to him.'

Joseph seemed to be on a roll and our silence allowed him to get his anger out of his system. 'I think Blatherley's days are numbered. In fact, we might get news of his sudden death within a day or two. What really pisses me off, though, is that somewhere in there, possibly in Number 10 itself, is a real snake.

I could name four or five, but there is one who is so dangerous that he could one day destroy the entire system of government. Corruption follows corruption until there is nothing holding the fabric together, and it all breaks up like dust, and there they'll be: All Honest Johns pretending to be as pure as the driven snow and blaming anyone who happens to be out of favour at the time.

'What are we doing, trying to rid the government of corruption, damn-well risking our lives and those of our friends, and for what? You tell me, for what?'

It was so unusual for Joseph to become so bleak. He had always been so positive. I thought all the killing was beginning to get to him. The sheer number of people who were willing to be assassins troubled him. I know for sure that he was fearless and not easily moved, but he also seemed to carry an inkling of pity or compassion for those who were now lying cold and bloodless around his garden.

Fran suddenly appeared at the foot of the stairs. 'Dick says that he's still a little hungry and he thought he could smell lentils and asked me to see if you had saved any for him.'

'Eddie, see if Dippy has finished with her bowl and take it up to Dick, will you?'

You can imagine the silence that followed. We all just stared until Merry, ever quick to get a joke, started laughing. It was then that we all got it and laughed with her. It was a welcome release.

Joseph continued with the next day's plans. 'I'm going to be up all night keeping watch. Tomorrow we will have to set up the rota. Merry, don't forget to call the rest of the gang and ask them to get here by tomorrow evening and tell them that they may be here for several days.

'Tomorrow morning we will have to sort out what we have in the way of munitions. Diana had better inform the local police to keep away despite any alarms being called. The last thing we want is a bunch of trigger-happy bobbies wandering around the garden taking bullets. By the way, where is Diana? Fran, is she with Dick?'

Fran returned from the kitchen holding Dippy's bowl. 'Yes, she's up there with him now, but ... is this all that's left?' A deep silence followed as she looked at each one of us, puzzled.

Diana had been with Dick and came down, apparently quite happy with his improvement. 'I hope this keeps up. He's looking so much better. It's a damn nuisance that I have to leave shortly. I think you could do with an extra gun. Do you want me to talk to MI6, Joseph? Or is that pushing it a step too far?'

'They'll only try to take over and make a thorough mess of it. I know them of old! Besides that, half of them would get bumped off and, of course, we are not quite sure whether they can be trusted or not. I think caution is probably the best option for the moment.'

Merry had slipped out and suddenly reappeared at the door. 'Won't somebody bloody well help me?' She was completely laden down with armaments. Tom stood and lent her a hand. Laid out, all told, there were five automatic pistols, fifteen ammunition clips, six knives of various sorts including a couple of cut-throat razors, half a dozen grenades and some other bits and pieces that she thought would be useful.

'Bunch of bloody Teddy Boys, if you ask me!' she declared. 'Anyone want a shave! What about you, Militant?'

'No thanks. I had one last week,' came the immediate, somewhat aggressive response.

'What about us all having some of your wine, Joseph?' When I said it, the words came out quite easily. It was the first time I can recall that I felt completely at ease in the company of people whom I had only recently met, Ada and Militant being the exceptions. It was a matter of really being there with them and not just as an onlooker scratching at the window to be allowed in. When you've lived outside society most of your life as I have, there's a tendency to be nervous about being too forward, if you see what I mean.

I suppose that the best way I can describe it is to imagine one is a cat living alone in the woods and suddenly discovering that there is a colony of animals living close by. The cat can see that they are very much the same but also senses that they have their own rules of how to get along together. So the best thing for the cat to do is sit and watch and avoid a scratched ear, if it can. In time, the rest of the colony will accept it and even allow it to eat from the same bowl.

It all takes time and, believe me, it is so easy for the animal to fall out of favour with the others for being too pushy. That's what it felt like. But in this case, it was really just something that was in my head and from which, even now, I can't completely free myself. Silly, isn't it?

I must say, though, that if Ada hadn't been there to keep me on course, I think I might have slipped away and back on the road a good while ago, right at the beginning of the adventure. It's all about grasping the concept of purpose and holding on to it and sometimes it's not that easy for me to do.

Joseph managed to come around a bit after his outburst. 'Come on, Ada. Let's get some supper sorted out before Eddie falls over. Merry, Militant, get the glasses. Tom, there's a case of champagne down in the cellar at the far end on the right. Bring up four or five bottles. We should celebrate that we have survived today's onslaught and can look forward to getting all this over and done with. Do you know, this is actually the biggest fight our whole organisation has had to deal with.

'Eddie, I don't know what they're after, but it strikes me that, even if there were a thousand tons of rhodium on your patch, it doesn't equate to the lengths that Blatherley is going to. I just can't think what it is.'

Joseph was right. The whole thing was growing into a real mystery.

Chapter 23

'Basilisk here. Are you free to talk?'

'Yes. What's going on?'

'Your idea of sending in MI6 on a ruse was a total disaster! Four innocent players were killed, for Christ's sakes! They managed to seriously wound target DR, but that's it. And who the hell are the clowns you sent in for the second round of circus antics? They couldn't even shoot straight and it got four of them killed!'

There was a silent pause on the other end. Finally, the Secretary of State spoke. 'Let this be the one and only time you speak to me with that tone of voice unless you want to join the dead-man gallery. Is that understood?'

Basilisk took a deep breath. 'I understand, but surely you can understand my frustration. I'm laying my life on the line for you and the organisation and the least you can do is provide competent enforcers who'll get the job done. Except for the two legal eagles, one of which has been put out of commission for now, and one female copper, the rest are just amateur mercenaries playing a dangerous game, yet the ones who are losing the contest are us. Are your people even aware of my presence there?'

'Yes, Basilisk, they're aware. I am told that your tracking device is relaying clear signals to them so they can identify you without giving you away to the enemy. Now tell me what's going on.'

'Let me first warn you that this last failed episode has only served to poke a rabid dog. They're more determined than ever to expose you and anyone associated with you. Obviously, that puts me in a very precarious position. Here's the thing. They know about your Russian connection. One of your Russian hitmen was wounded and taken alive.'

'What!' The Secretary sprang to his feet and began to pace the floor. Basilisk could hear the man's heavy breathing at his end. 'How much do they know?'

'Not much yet, but they will. Most likely he'll be interrogated, and with the chance to defect, he'll probably sing like a canary.'

'Can you eliminate him?'

'Negative. He's being watched like a hawk. Too risky. We'll have to deal with the consequences.'

'Dammit! We can't let this happen. We've got too much to lose.' For once, the Secretary seemed to be at a loss.

'Speaking of canaries, what's happening with Curtain? He's told them everything he knows. Is there a funeral service planned?'

'I'll be calling him directly and giving him an ultimatum. Now that he's in with Sphinx, he's in an excellent position to gather intel. Temporarily, that is. His days are numbered regardless. I'll need you to keep a close watch on what he does after I contact him. Anything else?'

'That's all for now.'

Chapter 24

Whoever invented the wheelbarrow was either a genius or a madman. I can imagine that the inventor had to make do with what they possessed, one wheel and a lidless wooden box to shift anything heavy when needed. Two or four wheels would have been better but when one has several bodies to move, then a wheelbarrow, if nothing else is available, will have to do. So Militant and I set to work, and soon we had the garden cleared with even more bodies propped up in the coach house.

The man that Militant shot was now inside with Fran who was trying to dislodge the bullet from his shattered ankle, apparently without anything to calm him. After the screaming had subsided, Joseph and Edyta entered the 'surgery'. Dick was in the process of uncovering his ears while the newcomer was busy wiping the tears from his face.

Fran had concluded her business, had reset a couple of broken bones, and had strapped the foot up so that it resembled an extremely large sock pulled over a wellington boot. Joseph had difficulty in suppressing his laughter and muttered to Fran as she left the room, 'Nice job, Fran!'

***

As nighttime drew on and a general quiet settled over the entire house, I started to think about my relationship with Ada. It was odd, the way she was so self-contained, so self-controlled, the way she knew how to do so much, you know, the guns and things.

While lying in bed that night, I got up enough nerve to talk to her about my feelings. That's a very odd thing for me to do, really. The only feelings I have ever felt for anything or anyone have been towards the animals who befriended me, but they never talked back though I sensed what they were thinking.

Then, of course, there was Marina, but that was short-lived when I learnt that she was my niece and I had to tuck away any improper feelings though I still care about her.

But this was different. Ada was a human being, just like me, who seemed to genuinely care about me, dare I say love me. I had never been in this situation before, but that night, I felt the courage to tell her what I was thinking.

'You know, Ada. Never in a million years did I think I would ever have a relationship with anyone, least of all someone like you. It's like we come from two different worlds: me, a loner by choice, no roots to speak of, content with just living with nature and avoiding people as much as possible; you, smart, inventive, fearless. And here we are building a life together. You have inspired me and I can't help but be amazed that you see something in me that I don't see.'

'Look at me, Eddie. I had been watching you for weeks, and the more I saw you, the more I realised that you and I had something in common. We were both very much alone and I knew that we both needed not to be. You have more courage than you realise and you have a heart of gold.

'Oh, Eddie! You are such a treasure! Anyway, here we are, involved in a dangerous predicament and at the same time trying to find our way together. We've both got new lives to lead now, hopefully in a much better position than we had before.'

I took a deep breath and said very quietly, 'Thank you, Ada, for accepting me into your life.' She smiled, got up, put her dressing gown on and left the room. I wondered if I had said something wrong, but then she returned with two glasses of Joseph's champagne and gave me a kiss on the cheek.

'You know, you've come a long way since we first met, Eddie,' she said, handing me a glass. I've got a feeling that inside your world of mysteries lives a thinking, sensitive person. And I'm really glad that we found each other.' She sipped from her glass and smiled.

'But Ada, you found *me*. You knew me long before I knew myself. Do you know, when you're on the road as I have been, all you can think about is where to find the next meal and where to spend the night. One never thinks about politics or holidays in the sun. It's just one day after another without any ambition except the means to survive.

'But now all that has changed and it feels so much better. I like being a person. I like to have thoughts that go beyond hunger. Do you realise that if it hadn't been for Marina, none of this would have happened; a cold, dead young woman who I wanted so much to live. She lost her life and gave me mine. Can you imagine what might have become of me in, say, ten years' time? I'd probably be a crumpled heap lying in a ditch feeding the eels.'

'Eddie, I would have rescued you long before that would have ever happened. Sometimes I think we were meant to be. Remember how we met, pitchfork and all? You were already in my sights.'

And that was that. Ada and I, totally caught up, connected, joined together. No one will ever know what that felt like to me. Not only that, to be closely entwined within her arms, her body pressed close to mine, was something that I had never experienced before, and it was sometime later that we finally fell asleep.

***

Morning arrived quietly. There was a slight sea mist that blocked out nearly all the sounds of passing ships and the rising tide. Ada came into the bedroom holding two cups of tea and a couple of petit beurre biscuits.

'Joseph looks completely washed out. He needs to sleep. I think we should go down and relieve him. '

We descended to the kitchen for breakfast joined by Militant and Edyta, Merry, Diana, Tom, and Fran. To our great surprise, Dick was sitting at the table looking somewhat tired but with a healthy colour in his cheeks.

'Dick, how good to see you up. You look wonderful!' Ada said as she lightly kissed his forehead.

'I feel pretty good, just a bit sore, but happy to be alive. I was just thanking everyone for their support. Your friendship means a lot to me. You too, Eddie. I heard you singlehandedly carried me over your shoulder like a sack of potatoes.' Everyone laughed and it felt great to see him in such good spirits.

Joseph, despite his total lack of sleep, was already thinking of the next steps we needed to take. 'We must question our prisoner to find out...'

Diana interrupted him. 'Joseph, go to bed! You are spaced out at the moment and you are not going to question anybody until you've had some sleep. The man is not going anywhere with that kind of injury and the information can wait, whatever it is. So go to bed as soon as you've eaten. We will keep watch, won't we, Merry?'

'Too right,' Merry said. 'Can someone pass me the scones?'

Joseph finally went off to his bedroom and we saw nothing of him for nearly ten hours which, for him, was akin to the sleep of the dead.

After breakfast, a few of us went to interrogate the injured Russian who was sitting up having his eggs and bacon. He stopped with his fork midway and stared at the bunch of us who strolled in, unsure of what was going to happen.

Edyta, like so many Polish people, knew a certain amount of Russian, and Diana thought it might be a good idea to make the prisoner feel a little more at ease. He was obviously nervous, so Diana instructed Edyta to tell him that we just wanted to ask a few questions and he could continue eating his meal. Speaking in Russian, Edyta obviously started with small talk because as she conversed with him, the Russian seemed to relax some.

After half an hour or so, she managed to drag out of him that, far from being a highly trained killer, he was no more than a grocer from Ukraine who was being pressured by the local Mafia to do as he was told or his family would suffer the consequences. He had unfortunately got into their debt by failing to pay the protection money that they demanded.

At Diana's request, Edyta asked him his name and to relate what was so important that all these attacks needed to take place. His answer was puzzling.

'Radioactive mercury! There are rivers of it just over there under a stretch of woodland. They say that it is the only natural source known. It's very costly to produce, so it must be worth a fortune. I understand that there is also a deposit of rhodium on top of the site and I believe that the proceeds from that would pay for the extraction of the mercury. That's why all these crooks are after it.

'I suppose I'm lucky to be alive. I understand that all the others who came with me are now dead. We were all in a similar position, held for ransom with no chance of escape. We were just the front runners, the decoys. The real heavies are coming soon and will be more difficult for you to pin down. We were never trained to fight, none of us, not like them. We're just ordinary tradespeople, not gunmen.'

Ada and I actually started to feel sorry for him, a victim just like we were. It became even more alarming how far-reaching Blatherley's evil tactics had become.

It certainly was depressing news. If only we had understood how desperate the opposition was, we might have been able to persuade those poor men not to throw their lives away. Blatherley's crew knew full well that this group would be eliminated. I think it was their method of testing our strength and obviously now they had the measure of it. This news was red hot, and Diana could hardly wait for Joseph to awaken.

It was just as well that Merry had called the rest of the gang, who had already started to arrive in ones or twos. We had them gather in the sitting room until all were present so that everyone could be made aware of what was to follow.

Merry had already gleaned more tit bits of information from the newcomers. 'Some told me that there was a lot of strange activity at the ferry embarkation room, not the usual ferry travellers. A lot of looking around, sort of checking out who else was travelling.

'Nina and Joe, a couple in the group, thought that they were of particular interest to an individual in a brown leather jacket who oddly walked past them at least six times while they were waiting to board the boat. Sam, another member, said that there were two other men who seemed much too interested in who was in the room, and they definitely weren't English due to their suntans. I don't think that counts as suspicious but it does to Sam.'

Merry continued, but some of it seemed, to Diana at any rate, a bit too made up. Altogether, our ranks had swollen to, I think, sixteen, leaving out Dick, of course. Diana told Merry to stop talking and lay out the weapons.

The dead in the garage had been a godsend in some ways in as much as they had added to the number of guns and ammunition that we now had in our possession. All told, Merry had accumulated enough for everyone to have one pistol and possibly twenty rounds each. There were also four grenades, but I wasn't convinced that anyone would have the chance to throw one, least of all Militant, what with his habit of looking at things with a child-like curiosity, not to mention his missing finger. I could just imagine what would happen if he took the pin out of a grenade. He would probably stand there looking at it until it took both his arms and head off.

We could hear Joseph's phone ringing, which was eventually answered and ended with a curt 'Sod off!' It was funny in a way because it was a phrase that was so out of character for him. But then again, he'd only just awoken. He joined us a few minutes later with a smile on his face.

'That was Blatherley. He told me to stop being a bloody fool and to back off before it was too late. He said that I should get Edward Dew to withdraw his claim on the land and then there would be no further trouble. I told him that he was not in a position to demand anything and that his days were numbered. Then he tried the old 'I'm warning you', so I told him to blank-off and hung up on him.

Joseph moved on. 'What's to eat? Who's doing the cooking tonight? There's a ton of stuff in the freezer. Any news from our prisoner yet?'

He was obviously back on form, and after he was told what the man had said, he took charge again.

'First of all, Eddie, don't let this bother you. It is no longer as much to do with your land as it is with corruption. Whether you decide to sign it all away or not is totally up to you. But in eliminating corruption in high places, we also do away with the obstacles that keep you from acquiring and enjoying what is rightfully yours.

'Now, let's get our Ukrainian friend in here for supper. I think he should be treated as an ally after what he's shared with Edyta. The thing is, do we give him a gun or not? Is he a comrade-in-arms for us or for the other side? I assume that we will have another visit tomorrow night. Tonight will be too soon for them to have re-organised.

'Diana, can you find out where Blatherley is because I think I need to pay him a visit after his call, if he's not too far away. Merry, I'll leave you to distribute the guns and share out the ammo. Tom, please give Merry a hand. After a pause, 'Come to think of it, it's been a long time since we've had a siege around here. The last time, I think, was the French around 1545.'

Later that afternoon, Edyta helped the prisoner, Dimitri Kirov, to join us all at the dining table.

'Edyta, please ask him for details. Does he know anything about the mercury. How it was discovered would be a good start.'

Edyta asked the question and the answer was surprisingly detailed.

'Some years ago, in the 1980s, Southampton District Council sank a bore hole into a core of hot material 1.5 kilometres below the earth's surface. This geo-thermal heat was used to reduce the cost of energy for quite a lot of businesses, a hospital, and a university.

'One of the scientists, now dead, had secretly discovered that part of the heat generated was from radioactive mercury which showed up on only a few of the samples he was given. He kept very quiet about it until he was on holiday near the Black Sea and was grabbed by a gang of criminals. His only chance to save his life was to offer them a deal regarding the mercury.

'The leader of the gang thought he could sell the information on in order to get into the good books of a much larger syndicate. He hadn't considered that, having imparted the information, he was then of no more use and also a loose-tongued liability to those whom he had sought to woo. The gang and its leader were wiped out, and the scientist found that he was then in the hands of new captors. They were not very nice to him and he was returned to the UK in a terminal condition having been poisoned by, of all things, radioactive mercury.

'His death was followed by an inquiry headed by a Secretary of State in the British government – Blatherley, we assumed – which concluded that he had died from natural causes.'

Edyta said, 'That is apparently all the information that he has, and he says that he is sorry he doesn't know anything more about what is going on. And he asked if he could have something to eat. He said that before we captured him, he hadn't eaten for two days. Is that alright? '

Just at that moment, Tom and Merry brought in three massive tureens. 'Vegetarian night! If anyone wants any blood, they'll find plenty of it in the coach house!' There was a general grimace on the faces of all except for poor Dimitri, who didn't understand a word but was probably desperate to eat something, anything.

Plenty more arrived on the table, and by the end of the meal, everyone had eaten enough to satisfy a herd of goats.

Joseph whispered to Diana, 'Is Dick well enough to stay down here? I need to talk to him, Ada, Eddie, Tom, and Merry. We need to get a plan sorted out and ready for action. Tomorrow, if you can get a bead on Blatherley, I will see what I can do to get rid of him. Please arrange all that, but quietly. Thanks, Diana.'

***

It was difficult to imagine what Joseph's house was really built for. Ancient it was and very well fortified, but what Joseph was about to show us was truly astonishing. At the back of the house was a small lawn within the boundary of the brook, but hidden away at the base of the wall were a couple of oubliettes. These were sprung by simple iron pull handles tucked away in small recesses just above floor level inside the house. They were disguised on the outside as old paving situated below the ground floor windows, and when one of the pulls was operated, anything on top would be jettisoned into oblivion or rather into the grated alcoves in the cellar.

He had apparently discovered these devices after removing some of the old fruit-wood panelling which had become too enticing for the woodworm to ignore. It was amusing that, also on the ground floor, there were a series of culverin ports which had now been filled in, obviously to stop the draft.

It made me wonder what it was in those days that required such defences. I had noticed the pull handles for the oubliettes when Ada and I had first arrived but what with the servant bells and copper saucepans, I thought it was all to give authenticity to the place. It's amazing how some things don't change over the centuries.

Joseph gave us instructions as to what we should do. Each trap was now fitted with a sensor pad which, when trodden on, would show up on a small red light secreted in the interior wall. Everything was connected to Joseph's monitor, and he would direct us to pull the levers as and when he demanded. As he had said, 'The success or failure of this rests on my shoulders,' and we all knew that we had to respect his wishes.

The last of the Wingeing Ninjas had finally arrived and had eaten, been shown their rooms, and were now gathered in the lounge along with our group.

'Merry, tell us about everybody. Names will do for the moment so we know who we are giving orders to.'

There were eight Ninjas altogether. How Joseph expected to remember them all I don't know, but he seemed quite confident.

Diana shared her latest update. 'Joseph, I've just heard that Blatherley is in Havant at the moment and is shortly to be showing a bunch of Russians around the naval dockyard. Bit stupid if you ask me. Are they Russians or a new bunch of punters for his schemes, I wonder?'

'It's a bit too far for me to go tomorrow. There's too much to arrange here. Are you still going back to York tomorrow, Diana? Will Dick be going with you?' I could see that Joseph was keen to see Dick out of the firing line, and it was obvious that Diana had to show up to her 'regular job', just to keep our cover. She had already spent far too much time away from it.

'Yes, we're catching the 10.00 am ferry, but I'll call you if we see anything out of order at the other end. Anyway, let's get everybody sorted out. Who's had firearms experience?'

Merry stepped up, clutching a pistol.

'Oh, Merry, we know all about you. I meant who among the rest of you has any kind of skill in firearms use. We need shooters and loaders.' The response was interesting but not terribly encouraging.

'I won a teddy bear at a fun fair,' said Joe. Joe was around fifty years old but looked about sixty. His skin was a little lax though he had been a weightlifter earlier in his life. When he stopped, his muscles slackened, and though still very strong, he had the appearance of looking a little worn out. Nonetheless, he'd won a teddy bear, which was a good start.

Griff had been a blacksmith and could do anything with a hammer, but as a loader, he'd be out of the question. He and his family were put in a bed and breakfast where they stayed for the next five months. Having lost the business and being given no compensation, their lives went steadily downhill until Griff met Joseph. The case that followed allowed the family to regain some of their self-respect and they were able to get started once again in Southampton.

Welsh, he loved Joseph's wine and didn't mind smelling of leeks, which ironically happened to be his favourite vegetable. He had fallen foul of a town planner who was responsible for demolishing his workshop where he, his wife and family lived and worked, replacing it with an Express mini market.

Maureen Dickens was promising. She was quiet to the point of being silent. She loved to play darts but was so good at it that no one would play against her, and as I mentioned before, she was a good shot with a Nordic walking stick. Her aim was second to none. But a dart or Nordic stick is not the same as a pistol or rifle. Needless to say, she was not going to be a loader.

Jill was once a police dog handler and chose to be a loader, having little confidence in her trigger finger after losing two of its neighbours to an over-enthusiastic Alsatian.

Merry had brought her daughter, Melanie, as her own personal loader. They looked so much alike that it was hard to imagine what her father might have looked like.

Alex and Arthur were a proper duo. They thought the same, dressed the same and, worst of all, had the same laugh, if that was the word for it. They had both been in the ATC as teenagers, both wanted to be pilots but ended up at the maintenance end of the air force. They left the service but carried with them a decent knowledge of weapons if nothing else.

'We'll take turns,' said Alex. 'You go first, Arthur.'

'No, you go first, Alex.' You can imagine the rest.

Joseph sighed deeply. 'Merry, Tom, please take the group down to my firing range and have them target practice. Ada said she's got plenty of ammo at her place, and we can always pop over there should we need to.'

All that was left was for Joseph to give us our positions, who was to be upstairs and who was to stay with the traps, but that was to be sorted out the following morning. The funny thing is that had the enemy arrived that evening, we would have had nothing in place, so it was just as well that nobody came.

I started to remember my life before I met Ada and, in a way, I missed it. It was so simple. I owned nothing except a bag of dog collars, and I owed nothing. It was just, well you know, uncomplicated. Now I had put on about ten pounds, was never that hungry, and was never really cold or wet as I had been before. But for all that, I still missed it.

Don't get me wrong. I would not have gone back to it. There were a lot of problems and people don't often understand why people like me should have ended up in that kind of situation.

As a result of that, some of them had been very abusive to me, called me names ... pisshead, waste of space, and worst of all and the most common, parasite. Bearing in mind that I had never received a penny that was not willingly given and never a sou from the state, I thought such comments were a bit rich. What's more, those who do give to charities often receive some kind of personal solace as recompense.

Now that things had changed, I was beginning to realise that there was a point to it all. It appeared that I was going to have wealth beyond all measure if we survived the following few days. On the other hand, we were dealing with a band of people who were driven by such extreme greed, people who already had more than enough on which to live very comfortably. So my resolve, keeping in mind that both Ada and I had no next of kin, was that whatever was left over would mostly be given to charity and some used to help Joseph and Diana and their backers to continue in their quest to eliminate corruption in high places. I asked Ada what she thought.

'Scribble it down, tonight, Eddie, and give it to Dick before he leaves in the morning. So if anything goes amiss in the next few days, your wishes will be dealt with as a last testament.'

Ada asked Dick if he could draw up a basic will, and together we thought up all the causes that we could support between us. The list was quite long and included the Salvation Army, which had always been a staff for me to lean on when things were really difficult. Though it was just a rough draft, Joseph witnessed it, and Dick gave it to Diana for safe-keeping until they got back to York.

It was a relief to get that sorted out because, whatever happened, Blatherley and his crew could never, no matter how many of us were killed, be able to claim the land that I owned. Do you know, having done that, I felt so much relief. I no longer had to worry about how to dispose of that wealth, if that is what one wanted to call it.

Everything suddenly stopped. There was music, dance music! It was as if the walls were going to crumble. Joseph had put an LP on his gramophone. Nobody had noticed it before, hidden in a corner and covered with books and other documents.

'Come on, you lot! Get up and start dancing, for tomorrow, we die!'

Nobody moved. We just looked at each other with a kind of suspicious questioning. Had Joseph gone completely mad or was it just the strain taking hold?

Ada pulled me up from my chair. 'Come on, my darling. This is our tune!' The thing was, though, that Ada and I didn't have a tune, least of all one from the 1930s, and it would have to be 'Happy Feet', wouldn't it? My god is that a tune to get your blood moving! It was only tripping on the rug that saved me from dying of laughter. To see Ada moving the way she did was like sitting on a missile just as it was being fired. As for dancing, I don't know about that! It was more like seeing two giant squirrels fighting over an acorn. But despite the lack of style, everybody joined in and the floor shook with the rhythm of so many shoes. 'Happy Feet' definitely hit the spot.

'Shall I play it again?' shouted Joseph when it finished after three minutes or so. The following number was much more moderate, but most of us had already taken advantage of the couches scattered around his vast lounge. There was no doubt about it. The temperature had gone up and spring was in the air.

'Eddie, do you feel like taking another look at your woodland tomorrow?' I could see that Ada was missing the open air, and I must admit, I felt exactly the same.

'Yes, why not?' I replied.

'Joseph, can we borrow your old car in the morning?' Joseph could see what was on Ada's mind.

'Looking out for trouble, are you, Ada? Yes, of course you can. Do you know where I keep it?'

'Dick said you keep it in your lock-up with the blue door behind the treacle factory over in Southampton.'

'No, that's now being used as a doll hospital for moth-eaten toys. It's run by a couple with extremely long beards. My lock-up is now behind the workshops on Carlisle Road. I'll give you directions in the morning and the keys are in the kitchen in the can marked with a musical symbol.'

'Yes, I spotted it when we first arrived. Not really that subtle, though, is it, Joseph?'

'Point taken, Ada. All I can say is be very careful. The pick-up after twenty is almost too much, right up to thirty when it starts to labour a little. By the way, make sure it's full. It tends to drink a lot of petrol despite its lethargy.'

I wondered at that moment if Ada was on a quest, and I actually felt a little scared. I could see she was out for trouble. It was written all over her face ... you know, excitement, the twitch at the side of her mouth slightly manic. I was beginning to understand who she was and realised that she needed to be back on the moors as soon as possible.

As the evening wore on and the dancing and jigging came to an end, Joseph suggested that we celebrate our family with supper and, for a change, some extremely fine claret.

'Special occasions demand terrific wine ... my last case of Haut Brion '64. I'd hate to die and leave that to be pillaged by Blatherley's lot. Eddie, Ada, Militant and Edyta, to the kitchen, please. Joe, come with me to the cellar. Merry and Nina, clear the table and lay out the silver cutlery from the case over there. Alex and Arthur, take care of the surveillance. Just keep an eye on the garden. Right, let's do it!' And so it was, an evening like the Last Supper, something to be remembered.

We were all just about to go to our allotted rooms when Joseph's phone rang.

'Is there no peace? God, 11.45 and somebody wants to chat!' Needless to say, he answered the call.

'Is that Joseph? Boris here. Boris Curtain, the county councillor. You remember?'

'Boris, yes, it's me, but you sound disturbed. Tell me, what...'

'Blatherley! He phoned me a few minutes ago and told me to get a move on and press for a compulsory purchase order on that piece of woodland. I asked him under what pretext and he said, "Just bloody well do it, or else!" What can I do?'

'Boris, can you fire a gun? If so, telephone him and tell him to go to hell and get yourself over here as soon as you can. Are you any good with a pistol?'

'I was a weapons instructor in the Royal Artillery years ago. I can probably pick up on that.'

'Where are you at the moment? Is there anywhere you can hide until the morning ferry? Get your family out as well, if possible. I know you have a problem with that, but there could be some serious reaction from Blatherley if you don't do as I suggest. If you want to hold out a bit longer, then just agree with him and tell him that you will do what you can. Either way, you've got a problem. He's going to have you killed whether you do as he says or not.

'Your best bet is to join us here and quickly. Call us when you've caught the ferry and we'll pick you up at the terminal. Second thoughts? Don't call him. Just come over here. Can you do that?'

***

We expected to see Boris the following morning, but he didn't arrive, and by noon, Joseph was getting a little anxious. Diana and Dick had left on the first ferry out and called in to say that everything seemed normal at the other end. But Southampton is a big place and one can only ever see a small part of what goes on there.

Joseph decided to call the council offices to see if there was any indication of Boris' whereabouts. It was almost to be expected. The news was bad, very bad. Boris, his wife, and their two daughters had all been killed when their car, travelling in the direction of the ferry port, was crushed by an overloaded scrap-metal lorry that was moving at high speed. The driver of the lorry survived, but the police refused to give any more details until an investigation into the accident was completed.

I could see that Joseph was devastated. He felt responsible for their deaths, and there was little that any of us could say or do to console him.

Ada eventually took him into his study and had a long chat with him which, though it didn't change any part of the tragedy, helped him to get a grip on the problem at hand. It was Blatherley's demands that started the whole thing anyway, and all the ifs would've never changed anything. If it wasn't Boris and his family, it might have been the school party in the minibus behind Boris's car. And none of us can go back in time.

The only good thing that came out of it was that Blatherley's demand on Boris had failed, which must have put him in a fairly critical position with his partners. He probably suffered some real problems in the very short term as a result.

***

It was just before dark, around six o'clock, when Diana called to say that they were back in York. During the day, she had tried to find more information on Blatherley from MI6, but they told her that there was nothing new on that score and that he was off their radar. She said that she was a little suspicious that he wasn't even being watched.

'I think you are on your own from now on, Joseph. I think that MI6 has been warned off, and if that is the case, I believe

Blatherley has been given free will to do whatever he wants. It's possible there are other government officials ready to grab a share of the proceeds if this thing goes through. There's not much more I can do from here at the moment. Good luck. I'll call tomorrow.' And she was gone.

'Listen everybody. It's on for tonight! I think we should get ready for the onslaught. It's going to be rough, and remember that they will not take prisoners. So don't indulge in any conversation if they want to talk!'

It was around seven when Dippy suddenly arrived, seemingly worried and looking over her shoulder at the cat flap as if something was chasing her.

'We have visitors, and it's barely dark. I'm going to shut down the lights just to show that we are ready. There's a rather unfriendly electric wire running around the garden which I shall activate intermittently to disorient them. So if you hear a scream, just shoot at wherever the sound comes from. The wire also activates a floodlight on that particular area, but they will probably shoot those out as soon as they light up, so bear that in mind.

'Listen! There's a boat approaching the jetty. Damn it! That's a bloody shame! I thought that was still a secret. Obviously, someone in MI6 has dropped the word. I wonder who that was, and I wonder how much that information was worth. It's a good thing I've booby trapped the approach.'

The flash from the explosion that followed Joseph's words certainly came as a relief. It seemed to all of us that nothing was left to chance, but what has always amazed me in all of that was that we never saw a sign of a policeman despite the fact that guns were being fired night after night in that corner of the island.

A sudden burst of automatic fire broke the tension, followed by a solitary *dum*. Ada had made her target with a single shot. She was muttering something I couldn't make out. Sensing that

I was watching her, she turned her head towards me and smiled. 'Don't mind me. I'm allowed to be grumpy sometimes.'

At that point, there was a thud at a window close by, followed by a plaintive, drawn-out, *'argh'*. Nina was spot on and had jettisoned another assailant down into ... actually, I never found out for sure where these devices emptied themselves. I thought it was to the alcoves in the cellar, but in hindsight, I didn't notice any openings in the ceilings down there. The thing is we never saw anything to clean up afterwards. All I know is that once gone, there didn't appear to be any further trace of the victim. So, what can one assume?

For an elite squad of highly trained killers, their performance was not what I would call brilliant. At one point, it was as if the enemy was indulging in some form of alternating end, as one would suffer electricity with a scream and another would take a tumble over a wire, and then another with a bullet. Anyway, it went on for about half an hour and then all went quiet. It was obvious that there were still several out there but I think they were at a loss as to how to get to us.

Joseph was pensive. 'Interesting. I think they've run out of strategy which gives us a chance to take the battle to them. We need to teach them a lesson. I'm going to activate the fence and turn the floodlights on in a few minutes. When I give the signal, start shooting, even if you have no target. The more lead that we throw out, the more they'll stay pinned down.

'We'll do this for just ten seconds and then stop. I'll douse the lights but leave the fence on, then after my second signal, we'll do it again and then again and again. I just hope we don't run out of ammunition in the meantime. Whatever they try to do, they will never know if they'll be caught out in the open.

'So, is everybody ready?'

We all nodded and Joseph gave the signal. It was fascinating! There was no return of fire at all. The second time, two had broken cover and were immediately taken down. The third time, another one fell.

A voice shouted out through a loudhailer, an English voice. 'Come on, Joseph! You can't win, you know you can't. You are outnumbered and eventually you'll run out of ammunition. What will you do then? Throw sticks at us?'

It was Blatherley. I thought that it was quite brave of him turning up for the fight.

There weren't many politicians who had the guts to do that. But there again, he had a lot to gain, or so he thought. I'm sure he thought that there wouldn't be any survivors or witnesses to give evidence against him.

I could see Ada searching the garden with a pair of small binoculars.

Blatherley's voice could be heard again. 'Look, Joseph, I'm not a greedy man! There's plenty there for all of us. All you have to do is—'

There was a single shot. The bullet passed straight through the loudhailer and into the throat of the speaker. Blatherley went down, his head thrown back in the most alarming manner. All I could think at the time was that the shot must've gone straight through the top of his spine. It was grotesque, but it was quick.

When I looked over at Ada, her arm was still outstretched, smoke drifting from the muzzle of her gun.

Total silence followed. None of us spoke nor was there any movement outside for ten minutes or so. And then a single voice called out from the garden, this time with an eastern European accent.

'We need to gather the wounded and then we will go. We will not return. You have killed our paymaster. No wages ... no soldiers. So please, no shooting while we take our friends and go.'

In the floodlight, we could see them checking the dead and helping those who were wounded to leave. They left Blatherley where he fell. He was not going to be their problem, that was for sure. We could hear their vehicles slowly going away, and we all took a deep breath.

For us, however, there was a dilemma: how to dispose of Blatherley's corpse. It was easy to get someone from MI6 to clean up the others in the coach house, but since Blatherley obviously had a spy operating in MI6, the situation had become not so convenient. Joseph called Diana on her mobile to explain what had happened.

'Diana, I think it's all over. We are okay, but we've got one of the dolphins, the biggest one, well and truly beached. It died this evening. Do you think we can tow it out into deep waters and let nature take its course or can you suggest an alternative? We don't want it to surface again to pollute the beach. It would be much too unsightly.'

She was quick to reply. 'It would be best, as you suggest, to tow it into deep waters where there are a few sharks. That way there will be little chance of it re-emerging on the south coast. I'll get Jim to give you a call. He's very keen on environmental issues and will be pleased to help you out. Did you manage to refloat the rest on the high tide?'

'Yes, you know what they're like. The stronger ones helped to get the poorly ones off the beach and it was good to see them leave without any problems. I look forward to hearing from Jim. Bye for now.'

And that was that. Joseph thought that any further problems would be unlikely that night but was keen to get rid of Blatherley's corpse just in case any of the government services might care to pay an early visit.

'Eddie, Militant, Tom, would you do the honours and get Blatherley down to the jetty? He's dead weight. That's the problem with these politicians. They get far too fat from the grease they use to line their coffers. Mind the steps. Oh, there are some large black bags that I left in the coach house. It might pay to slip him inside one. That's all he deserves anyway. Watch out for the debris from whatever blew up earlier. I wouldn't want you to slip on the blood!'

Joseph chuckled when he said that, though I thought it was sort of chilling, you know, a little out of place under the circumstances. But I supposed one could get like that in the kind of business in which he was involved.

'By the way, Eddie, I'm glad it was Ada who got him. You two have the most reasons to take some kind of revenge. Let's face it, he was responsible for both Ernest's and Marina's deaths, and if the truth were known, it would bring closure to so many other families who have suffered the consequences of his gluttony.'

I'm not quite sure how Ada felt at that moment. She was sitting in the comer, had taken her guns apart, and was carefully cleaning the barrels. She didn't look up as Joseph passed, but he turned back as he reached the door and whispered something in her ear. She said nothing, not a word, but just smiled.

She looked quite relaxed but I'm sure that there was something worrying her. I let it go for the moment. I didn't think it was the right time. I was sure that she would tell me what she was thinking later. And so she did.

'Eddie, you have to make a decision very soon, and it is very important that you understand the situation that you're in now. I mean fully understand. Blatherley is dead. There are and will be others who will take up the challenge to acquire, honestly or dishonestly, that piece of woodland. You don't want to keep it, do you?'

'No, not really,' I replied.

Ada took a deep breath. 'Okay. Have you thought about what you'll do?'

'I have a vague idea but I was hoping that you'd help me figure it out. There are so many pieces to this: the rhodium and mercury, the land, the properties on the land. I'd like to keep some for us and the rest to go to charities.'

Ada looked at me with a sort of curiosity mingled with a touch of surprise. 'Okay.' She thought for a minute, then said, 'Firstly, I think we need to find someone who can mine the rhodium and would be happy to be under contract to a consortium of worthy charities. Then when the rhodium is completely extracted, the proceeds could be used to drill for the mercury. Finally, all the proceeds from that after the initial costs are met can go to the consortium.

'So what charities did you have in mind? I know you had mentioned the Salvation Army.'

'Well, I'll need a little help on this, but definitely Médecins Sans Frontières, the Red Cross, Save the Children, Mencap and Greenpeace. What do you think?'

'Eddie, you couldn't do better than that, but the problem is that you will still be the owner of the land.'

'I thought I could give the land to them as soon as they got together. I might be dreaming but I don't think that they could refuse an offer like that, especially if the gift is publicised. That way, no one could challenge them. Also with Greenpeace, I would have to check if they would want anything to do with radioactive mercury.'

Ada seemed pleased that I had already worked something out. 'Sounds good to me. Speak to Joseph in the morning. You will need to make contact as quickly as possible because it's bound to take a few months to get them all together, what with accountants, advisers and the like. Get Joseph to call Dick and ask him if he can start to work on it. The will that you gave to Dick still stands and will need to be altered as soon as there is a proper plan in place.'

I could see that Militant and Tom were still waiting and getting a little impatient, so I gave Ada a quick hug and off we went to half-drag, half-carry the fat man onto the wheelbarrow and then down to the jetty. The wheelbarrow was apparently not the thing to use.

Blatherley's head seemed to be held on only by the skin of his neck, and being so loose, we were bothered that it might come off as we took him down the steps. We decided to tie his body onto a plank with one length of rope, and his head with another piece. It was really quite good because the three of us, despite Militant being only one-handed, found it easy to slide him, step after step, down to the jetty. We left him there still tied to the plank, in a state which one might describe as stiff.

Chapter 25

It was around five the next morning when the boat arrived. 'Only one this morning, Joseph?' Jim was Diana's personal environmental resource to whom she had given Joseph's contact information for assistance.

'Actually we have quite a collection, but there's only one who really needs to vanish. What have you got in mind, Jim?'

'Lobster beds. Hungry little devils! I'm going out to put some pots down this morning, so it's an ideal chance for him, them, and us, not that he'll appreciate it. What I don't catch tomorrow will be a lot fatter in a fortnight, if you follow my reasoning.'

Joseph liked Jim's idea. 'It sounds good to me. Have you got enough weights or shall we sort that out here before you leave?'

'Nah! Don't worry about that. He won't be coming up, rest assured. Usual rate?'

'Yes, of course, but don't say any prayers over him. He's not worthy. That carrion's responsible for the deaths of a lot of innocent people and that doesn't even include his associates. We definitely don't want him coming back to life in any form, not even as a fish.'

Jim laughed. 'Okay. Have you got anybody there to help me load him onto the deck or is it too early for your lot? I thought I'd better come on my own today. Don't want any prying eyes or loose tongues, do we?'

***

I had heard the soft *put-put-put* of the boat engine as it approached the jetty and slipped out to check that there was no trouble looming. I had awoken Militant, and together we cautiously approached the inlet. It was then that we heard

Joseph's voice and the latter part of their conversation. I called out, 'Joseph, it's Militant and me, Eddie. We're coming down.' Once we were there, Joseph introduced us to Jim.

'Hello, you two! This is Jim. His father was once a drain technician.' Militant and I looked at each other, puzzled.

'Sorry, Jim, it's a bit early in the morning for these two and they had a heavy day yesterday.' After the penny dropped, Militant started to laugh. 'And I suppose your second name's Rodney, is it? Glad to meet you, Jim.'

We both shook hands with Jim, who seemed like a nice enough fellow.

'How long are you going to be out for, Jim?' Joseph asked.

'Oh, about twelve hours today, I suppose. Why?'

'Do you need any help? What about you two, do you want to go?'

Militant was happy to oblige, but I remembered that Ada wanted to go for a car ride, and since I was no kind of sailor, I felt it would be better for me to stay with her.

In next to no time, the three of us got on with the task of shifting the overweight carcass of the dead politician down into the boat. Once on the deck, I helped them hide the body under a tarpaulin. Soon the *put-put* of the little diesel engine faded into the distance, carrying the remains of a most unpleasant individual to its final oblivion.

Apparently, all went well for Militant and Jim. Militant was sick only once, and that was after eating one of Jim's sausage sandwiches.

Ada was already up when I got back and desperate to catch the first ferry. We had a quick breakfast and then left to retrieve Joseph's car. I'd never been in a really fast car before, but looking back, I think I'd only ever been in four cars in my entire life. Dick's motorbike was different. Ada was really careful on the roads, especially if they were wet. But this was going to be a lot different.

From the ferry terminal, we took a cab to the end of the road where Joseph kept his car. From what he'd said, I thought that we were going to be met with an old banger, but instead we found a rather dusty but very expensive Maserati sports car. At first sight, I thought maybe Ada was about to bite off more than she could chew, but after a trial run around the town, she headed out onto the motorway and put her foot down.

I was terrified. It was okay up to about 80 mph, but then, *whoosh!* The car took off like a rocket and it was only the acceleration that stopped my breakfast from doing a quick exit. I heard Ada softly exclaim, 'Wow, I love it!' Needless to say, I was totally unable to agree with her. Soon, we returned to normality and took the road headed to Havant and on to my extremely valuable woodland.

As we approached, we saw that some new fencing had been put up. We also noticed a partially built service road, a newly erected cabin and a small security hut which sat by the side of the gate.

'Right, just as I thought! They've done it again. They never give up, do they? Eddie, could you pass me my bag? I'm going for a little walk. Stay here, keep the engine running, and open the door when you see me coming. Take this, and if there is a problem, use it. I know you can. Okay?'

She got out of the driving seat, leaving one of her pistols on my lap, and walked straight up to the gate. I heard her mutter something to the security guard who, interestingly enough, didn't look into her bag. I saw her approach the newly erected cabin and was out of my sight for about two minutes before she calmly walked back towards the car.

At the gate, she said something to the guard who turned quickly and started to walk off towards the hut. It was then that I saw her drop something and run for the car. Once inside, she hesitated for a moment and then, *woosh!* We were away once again.

Within seconds, there was a terrific explosion, followed quickly by a second, but now we were far away from the site and heading towards Portsmouth.

'Ada! What was that? Where are we going now?' I asked.

'To have some lunch, of course! Aren't you hungry?'

As we reached our destination, I realised that I was still clutching the pistol.

'Eddie, give me that. Are you trying to get us arrested?' I sat there with my mouth open. She just laughed.

'We've got some living to do, haven't we, Eddie? Come on ... lunch!'

As we sat there in the sunshine at a table outside a not-too-plush restaurant, I asked Ada where she learned to drive like that.

'Playground duty on the Isle of Man', and that was all she had to say. I gave up for the moment because lunch arrived along with a bottle of rather indifferent white wine.

'You don't have to drink it, Eddie, nor do I. It smells not so much of gooseberries but more like cat pee. Besides that, I'm driving.'

As we left and paid the bill, we were handed a questionnaire regarding the meal.

Ada wrote, 'Nice spot in the sunshine, but please provide a proper pee receptacle for your cat,' and popped it into the box by the door. We returned the way we had come and passed by the entrance to the woodland. There was an ambulance and a couple of police cars blocking the entrance.

'What did you say to the guard?' I asked Ada.

'I told him that I was Blatherley's auntie and that I was leaving him a cake for his birthday, as I always did. On the way out, I told him that there was a little something waiting for him too.'

'I take it you didn't like him too much?'

'Yes. I recognised him as a doorman at a certain London hotel who pushed me down a flight of stairs when I was protesting against the fur industry about twenty years ago. I'm certain it was the same guy. In fact, I'm absolutely sure. Anyway, that's another old score settled.'

It wasn't long before we were back on Carlisle Road, parking the car in the lock-up and taking a cab to the ferry. We had time to enjoy peace for a few days by the sea before we made the return trip on Dick's motorbike to York, and then to Ada's solitary little farmhouse tucked away on the moors. It seemed almost like an anti-climax at the time, but Ada and I needed to share some time together to seal our relationship and get used to living without Joseph's garlic-scented wine.

Jim and Militant returned not long after us, and despite the choppy waters, Militant looked quite rosy. Edyta was relieved to see him return and hurried him away to make sure he was okay.

Dimitri Kirov was another problem for Joseph. It was obvious that the man was completely innocent of collusion with Blatherley's gang. But it was necessary to contact the next of kin of his comrades, offer condolences and possibly some kind of compensation. Joseph would have to discuss that with the society, but it was never going to be easy. Edyta would have to be there when the time came.

In the meanwhile, Militant had spotted a Russian freighter anchored not far out from the Solent. He had seen it as he returned with Jim from deeper water and mentioned it to Joseph later in the evening.

'There's a Russian boat out there just past the Needles. What do you think about asking the captain if he'd be willing to return the Ukrainian bodies to a Black Sea port? It would save a lot of bother for everyone.'

Edyta translated the conversation to Dimitri, who suddenly looked horror-struck and started to talk very fast, so much so that even Edyta had trouble keeping up with him. She turned to Joseph. 'He says that the captain is one of Blatherley's lot and will throw the bodies overboard once the ship is out to sea, just like he did to one of them on the way to Britain.

'On board his ship were wooden cases of wine, Mukuzani from Georgia, and some very old Tokaj from Hungary. But it wasn't wine in those cases. It was something else. The man who was killed had tried to bring one of the boxes of Mukuzani up to us from the hold. But one of the crew saw him, and then the captain shot him as he came up the stairway and had his body thrown into the sea.

'When he was shot, the man dropped the case, and the lid split open. There was no wine inside, just several large packets stuffed with white powder, two of which fell out onto the deck. One of the crew quickly gathered them up and took the box back down into the hold.'

It was at this point that Dimitri produced a piece of card from his trouser pocket and handed it to Edyta. It was a rather creased shipping address label. Edyta gave it to Joseph.

'My God! That old bastard was smuggling as well and using a government-bonded warehouse to store the stuff. This needs to be checked out! Look at this...'

The label read:

Ian Blatherley
Secretary of State for the Environment
House of Commons Wine Club Account
Western Docks Customs Bonded Warehouse
Southampton, United Kingdom

Edyta continued, 'Dimitri said that he found the label under the stairs the day after and believes it had fallen from the top of the wooden case. He says also that the captain is probably waiting to collect the other gunmen to take them back to Russia because the cargo was unloaded the same day as Dimitri and his colleagues disembarked. The others will probably go back to the ship by motorboat, he thinks.'

'Edyta, ask him if the others came to Britain by air?' Joseph inquired.

'Yes, he thinks that they came by plane, arriving at different destinations and collected their weapons from somewhere in London.'

'Diana is going to be pleased with this. It might be said that her sojourn in the south was all worthwhile.'

Armed with that information, Joseph telephoned Diana, and within an hour and a half, she called back to tell us that the ship had been seized, the captain and crew held. She also said that Customs and Excise was checking into all of Blatherley's holdings of imported goods wherever they could find them. We were all glad that this last episode was outside our sphere of operations.

Diana was highly commended for her work, and from then on, there was no further interference into Joseph's business by Special Branch or MI6. He continued monitoring the movements of various individuals in the government and brought together sufficient force to eliminate many of those whose practices carried them outside the bounds of justice. It struck me that wherever there is power there is also corruption, from the school playground right up to the government of the day. I hadn't thought much about it before, but those last few weeks at Joseph's had certainly put it right up there in the front of my mind. It was really quite depressing because no matter how many of these crooks were removed, destroy one and ten more would rise up to replace them.

I could see that Ada wanted to get back to being Ada Gampe, living on the moors. We both agreed that all that had happened over the last few months had left us, and me in particular, in a state of total confusion. When she took me in, I knew little about living with other people and then suddenly there I was in the midst of a group, each one of them slightly out of kilter with general society. But every single one was a genuine person with only goodwill and honesty to offer Ada and me. Friends like that are hard to find and harder still to keep. We were all, then, in the same boat, at the end of an adventure, and all feeling the same kind of anti-climax. Only a few days before, we were at an elevated level of nerves, and suddenly, we had to accept that it was all over and done with. At least that episode was, anyway.

Joseph was satisfied that we had reached the end of that particular chapter, and we all sat down for our last supper together, not knowing whether some of us would ever see each other again. That night when everything was done and cleared away, we slipped off to our rooms to pack our stuff ready for an early departure the next morning. Only Militant and Edyta had to stay to take care of Dimitri and to help Joseph deal with the bodies that were slowly inflating in his coach house. The rest of us would go back to our respective homes, wherever they may have been.

***

It was a grey morning with a lank, cold mist hugging the sea. The sun was struggling to break through but there was a promise of a better day ahead. At the Southampton terminal, we warmly embraced each other, exchanged contact details, and bid each other farewell. Soon, Ada and I were travelling north towards our new life together.

The road seemed almost without end, but eventually we reached York and called in at Dick's home. Diana was there, and together we shared our thoughts on the last few months. Diana explained how difficult it was to keep one side of her employment from interfering with the other. She had been trying to engage MI6 in identifying the mole who had been dealing with Blatherley. But she said she had to be careful for fear of blowing some of the secrecy of her and Joseph's agency, which may have already been compromised.

I spoke with Dick, whose wound was healing surprisingly well, and told him about our ideas for the plot of woodland. He was happy to work with Joseph to get something going, but as he said, 'Finding an honest, unaffiliated mining company to do the initial drilling for the rhodium will be difficult.'

It was then that I remembered someone I had met on the road years before. I knew him as 'Digger' Jim Cuttance. One of his great, great grandfathers had been a gold miner in Australia at Ballarat and had been killed by the British army. Digger had come back to visit his family home at a place in Cornwall called Gunwalloe on the west side of The Lizard and talked about getting started as a tin miner. If he had managed to do it, I felt sure that he would be willing to take on the work.

Dick said that he would try to track the man down. I suppose that it was about a month later that he told us he'd had some success. It was the first step achieved. The rhodium was one thing but to deal with radioactive material was another.

***

'Dick, do you think we should have told them?'

'I don't know, Diana. I think that the less people who know of our suspicions, the less potential for leaks. Plus, I don't really want Ada and Eddie to get any more involved in this muddle than what they've already been through. The evildoers involved might be tempted to interrogate them and it's best that they show genuine ignorance of the matter if confronted.'

'Yes, I agree on those points. It'd be disheartening for anyone, but especially Ada and Eddie, to know that one of our close friends has been operating as a mole for the other side. Whoever it is has done an expert job of playing both sides without detection. I've gotten nowhere with MI6 and it's possible that some who are privy to inside information might be covering up for him ... or her. I'm talking about staff at MI6 who would most likely be approached by the mole for intel.'

'You're right, Diana. The question then becomes, how do we suss them out? They would have much to lose, up to and including their lives, if anyone found out that they turned into informants. What could we possibly offer them to make the risk worthwhile? Would the witness protection programme be an option?'

'Yes, I thought of that as well, but not knowing where the double crossers are, we'd have no way of guaranteeing the informant and their family a safe passage with a new identity. Look at what happened with Curtain. I firmly believe that Blatherley planned that accident with information provided by our mole. Now that Blatherley's dead, I wonder what the infiltrator's next step will be.'

'That's a very good question, Diana. Unfortunately, that's yet to be seen as I'm sure we haven't heard the last of them yet. It's getting a bit late so I suggest that we sleep on this. Tomorrow, we should sit down and list all of the people who were involved with us, bar none. Let's take a closer look at their personal and work history and how each managed to infiltrate our group. Then we'll go from there.'

***

The following morning, we bade Dick and Diana farewell and were off to the farmhouse. What we encountered as we neared the farm was alarming. With guns drawn, we quietly walked around the perimeter of the property, intently listening for any sounds that might alert us to intruders. When we were fairly satisfied that we were alone, we carefully inspected the damage.

The barn was almost completely destroyed. It was then that Ada explained to me that beneath the barn was a cellar which she had used as her arsenal workshop. 'Eddie, before we left, I set up a booby-trap just in case the entrance was found. I didn't want anyone to make use of my stash had they found it. I'm really sorry that I didn't tell you but I didn't want to alarm you.'

'To be honest, Ada, I'm not bothered that you didn't tell me. But this is a bit shocking.'

Looking beyond the cellar's entrance, we could see that Ada's arms and supplies were intact beneath a thin layer of dust and debris.

The house was in a real state and was going to take weeks to restore. What was really annoying to Ada was that Wragge had left his fag ends all around the house, and the lavatory smelled worse than a shop doorway.

I was a bit concerned about the idea of intruders having invaded our personal space and the possibility that they might return. 'Ada, I'm wondering if this has anything to do with Blatherley's goons wanting revenge or if this was just some random burglars looking for stuff to steal.'

'Eddie, you are such a worrier! Just leave it to me.'

It was only when we unpacked our bags that I could see Ada was ready to carry on with her work. It was the grenades, two of them, which suddenly appeared on the kitchen table.

'What are you going to do with those, Ada?'

'Well somehow, I have to take them apart. I need the explosives to reload the brass casings that we used in the guns before we left. It's not that easy to come by good quality explosives these days. I've asked Joseph to send me details of how to dismantle them.'

I shuddered at the thought, but she seemed totally unconcerned. She looked up at me and said, 'Eddie, I'd like you to have one of my vintage pistols. I know I shouldn't break the pair, but at least they'll not be far from each other. They belonged to my great grandfather and were given to him for services rendered when he commanded a gunboat in the first great war. I was told that they were a pair of Navy Colts, but I don't know any more about them than that.'

'Ada, I'd be honoured, but you'll need to show me how to use it.'

'Of course. We can do some target practice once we get the house repairs sorted out.'

***

Dick and Diana called in regularly to update us on civilisation, and by September of that year, Dick had managed to sell our houses to the tenants in Southampton at extremely beneficial prices to the tenants, around two-thirds of their market value. That gave Ada and me some £400,000 plus the other half million to live on in as much comfort as people like us could ever wish for.

Dick also told us that the newspapers reported that the missing Secretary of State for the Environment was last seen leaving Kiev Airport arm-in-arm with a twenty-four-year-old Russian trapeze artist. I never knew how that news was acquired, but apparently his wife was reported to be concerned, not for his safety but the assurance that he was gone for good. The supposedly scorned wife was quoted as saying, 'Well, all I can say is good riddance to him, and to her, I hope you don't catch a dose of something nasty from the old dog, my dear!'

A good while later, my old acquaintance Jim Cuttance, who had agreed to mine the rhodium, paid us a visit after speaking with Joseph. He told us that the metal had paid him very well and that it had put him in a much better position to return to Cornwall to buy and upgrade the tin mine which, he said, had been his greatest ambition to own. He had sorted out with Joseph a charitable trust with 50 percent of the proceeds from the rhodium.

We were touched that Jim had travelled all the way from Cornwall to Yorkshire to personally thank us for giving him the means to set himself up. But he also informed us that there was not as great amount of the mineral there as was originally thought. The earlier assessment had been over-optimistic, but there was enough for him, the small workforce that he employed at the site, and the trust. It had also paid for the initial drilling to uncover the mercury. And that was the problem. There was none!

The metallurgists on site had asked for a copy of the original documents relating to the discovery in Southampton. They realised, after not finding in the text any scientific proof nor evidence that samples containing the mineral had ever been collected, that the whole thing had been an extraordinary hoax.

'Yes,' he said, 'there was some radioactivity present but not from any traces of mercury. In writing the secret documents, the author had given validity to the idea that there really was accessible radioactive mercury below the rhodium. That, in turn, had summoned his torture and untimely death. It was the secrecy that drew all the greed to the surface, and with it, the killing of so many innocent people.'

So many had perished, Ernest and Marina to start. Others were civil servants caught up in Blatherley's corruption. Then there was Oscar and three other members in the Southampton council offices who were thought likely to object to what was going on. The last three were run down outside a restaurant by a runaway transit van. It was a nasty and very sordid affair. The driver apparently suffered an asthma attack and was never taken to court despite witnesses claiming that they saw him aim his vehicle at the three diners.

And then, of course, one mustn't forget poor Boris Curtain and his family. Blatherley received a punishment far less than the one he deserved. Nothing could have lessened the trauma that he had inflicted on so many families. And his death did nothing to compensate me for the loss of both Ernest and Marina. The present news made all those deaths even more tragic.

There was nothing there! No millions to plunder, just a trail of death, and for what? Greed!

Despite Blatherley's demise, his grubby cold hands still clutched the tails of our coats, and it seemed that the contamination would be with us forever.

Chapter 26

Ada and I were married, which gave us the ideal opportunity to invite all our new friends to the farmhouse for a celebration, not just of our wedding, but of all that we had achieved together.

Merry brought in her new car an assortment of guns which she had acquired from a fisherman who had found them in his nets off the south coast. They had been dumped out at sea by the police after a gun amnesty some years before. They all needed a certain amount of restoration which she felt sure Ada could do in her spare time.

Merry also hinted that possibly Diana and I could set up a new cell to combat the evils that lurked around our part of the countryside. It was a thought, but the idea of blighting the peace around our patch of moorland with the sound of gunfire didn't appeal to us. Ada enthusiastically accepted her wedding present, which pleased Merry no end.

Joseph gave me a carton of his latest vintage, complete with the garlic edge, and to Ada he gave an antique dagger, its ivory hilt carved with the head of Medusa and the blade inscribed with the letter A. It was a fine present which she still treasures above all the rest. There were other gifts and homemade food. For entertainment, Militant sang several saucy folksongs to the accompaniment of Edyta's zither—a curious combination—but it was good and well meant.

After the joyful celebration and three days of walking and talking, Ada and I were left alone to settle our lives into some kind of order. But it wasn't to be so simple.

***

It was about a month after our wedding that I spotted a man and his dog down by the riverside not far from where I had kept

Marina hidden. I watched him for a while and noticed that he was running his dog in and out of the bushes as if he was trying to flush something out. Ada and I had bought from a retired farmer quite a large tract of that area which was still classed as agricultural land in order to preserve the peace and harmony that both of us treasured. One thing was for sure, though; we didn't like uninvited guests. I slipped out and circled around to his position, then stood looking down upon him from the bank above the river.

'What are you doing here?' I demanded in as commanding a tone as I could muster.

'What's it to you?' came the curt reply. I didn't like that too much, and I liked it even less when he pulled the stock and barrel of a shotgun from under his jacket. Pointing the gun at me and without any warning, he set his dog on me.

I've been bitten a few times in the past, having been a canine target for no apparent reason, but now as the owner of the land that I was standing on, the last thing I had in my mind was to run away. As the animal closed on me, I gave it a hefty clout on the side of its nose which sent it sprawling.

Once again, I demanded even more vigorously, 'What are you doing here? Don't try that stunt with your dog again unless you want it dead!'

The dog had run back to its master, who decided to respond to my question with a threat. 'There are cats here, and I'm shooting them whenever I see them. This area is for game birds and is part of the Blatherley estate, and I'm not going to let any manky cats destroy my livelihood!'

'That's where you're dead wrong, you twit! I own this property and you're trespassing. You injure one of my animals and you'll be sorry. Now, leave!'

To prove his value to the community as a preserver of the environment and seeing a heron passing over the trees, he suddenly aimed and fired, bringing the poor thing down, still flapping one of its wings in a desperate but vain attempt to escape.

I was furious but also speechless. I had met people like him before and had vowed that if I ever met another one, I would have to do something about it ... but what? I had no weapon on me.

My options were limited. My attitude towards aggression had changed quite dramatically over the last few months, and I found myself much more determined not to be cowed by uncompromising circumstances. Ada and Joseph had taught me a great deal and my mind had become much more focused.

I thought a ruse was my best bet, when I noticed lying quite close to the heron, a spiked, old, and well-rusted iron fence post. I slipped down the bank and moved towards the heron as if I wanted to give some aid to the dying bird, an act which attracted the man's attention. He moved forwards, driven by a disbelieving curiosity, having met somebody whose lust for wildlife blood didn't match his own.

His guard was down for that split second and never again was it to rise. He barely made a sound as the rusted spike pierced through his belly and upwards under his ribs.

Ada had heard the shot and hurried towards the sound. She had witnessed what had happened, and together we stood over the body of the man, not altogether certain as to our next move.

'Well, Eddie, you've certainly done it now, haven't you! I think you'll have to get that piece of old iron silver plated, maybe in rhodium, and inscribed with a runic inscription, something like *Creidhne Tuatha Dé Danann*. He was an iron worker among the Fey people, you know, and probably left that spike lying there just for you!'

I looked at Ada for a moment. What on earth is she talking about?

'Of course, that's what it was! They are here, you know. They like the water. Remember the storm and the lightning bolt? That was them, just as it happens when you are called to aid an animal on the moor.'

She seemed totally unconcerned about the actual event. There I was having just killed somebody and she thought it was funny. I didn't know whether to weep or throw up. But the fact remained that the man was intent on killing our cats and wildlife and that was something I could not allow. The irony of it was not lost on me. I had just killed a human who threatened to kill my animals. But in my mind, there was a big difference. Animals may kill for survival. He killed innocent animals for sport. Not only that, he seemed to be a real piece of work, above the law, threatening, disrespectful of other people's property. Maybe I did the world a favour. I didn't want to give it any more thought.

Ada's interruption was well timed. 'Eddie, he has to disappear double quick because he will be missed. Marina's grave is still there waiting for an occupant.'

I was loath to do it. In fact it was a sacrilege to use it, but it was empty and unused. It was too good for him but it did satisfy our immediate need. Would Marina ever forgive me? After all, it was for her, in the best possible, most beautiful place, now to be occupied by a callous, uncouth piece of shit! Somehow it just didn't seem right.

Ada read my mind. 'Eddie, you've got no choice. Come on, let's get it done. I take it the bird's dead now. Even that will have its purpose, poor thing.'

Ada returned to the house and fetched a rope from the barn along with a couple of shovels and a tub of quick lime. She tied the corpse's ankles, and together we dragged the body along the bank to the waiting grave.

'D'you know, Eddie, you did a damned good job with this hole. I hadn't really looked at it before. The police didn't see it, did they?'

I wasn't too sure, but I didn't think they had gone along the bank that far. We rolled the body into the hole, which fell with quite a loud thud as it hit the bottom.

'He doesn't look very comfortable, Ada,' I said, feeling just a bit guilty that I had killed him so horrifically.

'Never mind that, Eddie! While you sprinkle the lime over him, I'll go fetch him a pillow. Okay? He'll sleep better then.' I remember looking at her as she started to shovel earth onto the dead man. 'Come on, Eddie, get moving!' she growled. 'The sooner this is done, the better!'

It took us about two hours to fill the hole that took me four whole nights to dig. Ada plucked most of the feathers from the dead heron, and with a certain amount of debris from under the bushes and trees, she stamped the mixture into the still loose soil until the site looked untouched but for an old fox-kill, that being the heron.

Ada gathered up any property belonging to the gamekeeper, including his shotgun and cartridges, and hid them in her cellar.

***

Four days had passed before the police arrived. I'm not sure whether I was pleased to see Richards again or not. I think Ada was in the same frame of mind. But there he was with one of his companions who had obviously spent the trip in Richards' car deeply relaxed in the arms of Morpheus. Nonetheless, Richards was wide awake with the look of a worried man, never sure of what was really lurking behind the scenes up at Ada's farmhouse. He still remembered the morning after the storm.

'Hello again, you two and ... er ... I know it's a bit belated but congratulations.'

We passed the first ten minutes or so chatting about the weather and so on until finally he asked, 'Do you know or have you ever met your neighbour, Martin Jenkins? His dog was found yesterday. It had been run over. The thing is we don't know if it was done on purpose, in which case it is possible that something nasty has happened to its owner, or if Jenkins has just gone away and left his dog to its own fate.'

'Would you and your friends like a cup of tea?' Ada asked.

'That would be nice, thank you.'

I could see that Ada was having trouble keeping a straight face and needed to get out of sight to compose herself. I must say I was glad that she had walked away. It made it a lot easier for me to appear calm yet interested in what Richards had to say.

'Now the thing is, have you lost any cats around here?'

'Not that I know of. Ours were all here for breakfast this morning. Why?'

'Well, Mr Jenkins has been selling cat pelts to a fur dealer up north and selling the carcasses to an iffy restaurant somewhere in Leeds, both of which we are investigating at the moment. The thing is that no one who lives on or around the moors has lost a cat recently. The word is that Jenkins, who's a gamekeeper on the Blatherley estate, is the one who is taking them. If you see him, give me a ring, but don't tackle him. He has a shotgun which he conceals under his coat and we know that he's already taken a pot shot at some kids on the other side of Castleton.'

Ada had returned with the tea, and after a light chat about local gamekeepers' bad habits, Richards suddenly changed the subject.

'By the way, now that Blatherley's off in Russia, his wife has put the estate on the market, divided into 1,000 one-acre plots. If you are interested, give her a call. Her number's in the book. I believe that there is one part which runs right up to the edge of your patch and along the side of the National Trust, you know, where that car was burned out. If you've got the money, you'd do well to get a few plots.

'Apparently, there's a possibility that now that Blatherley's out of the picture, some of it could be used for a wind farm. I know some people don't like them but they are a lot nicer to look at than a nuclear power station, don't you think? Anyway, we had better be off now. Thanks for the tea. Oh, I nearly forgot to tell you. Sergeant Wragge committed suicide. Threw himself off a cliff on the south coast. Bye for now.' And off he and his companions went.

It was almost impossible for us to keep straight faces and it was just as well that they left when they did.

'Do you trust him, Eddie? I don't think I do.'

It's true. The old sayings 'once bitten...' or 'a leopard never...' are always worth remembering. But there was one positive thing about his visit and that was my justification, unplanned as it was. Jenkins was dead and a dammed good thing too by all accounts. Justice had been well served.

'Ada, what was the other policeman up to when Richards was talking?'

'He were poking around in the brazier out there and found the remains of your old plimsol. Remember that? They've taken it away in a polythene bag along with the string you had around your waist. I don't think that will get them very far. Besides that, all the bits that came from Jenkins are now recycled down in my workshop except for the shotgun butt, which we burned in the stove last night.'

I thought, *Hmmm, I wonder what they were looking for.*

Chapter 27

The prospect that Ada and I could become owners of part of Blatherley's huge estate was quite exciting. There were a couple of snags, however, that immediately came to our attention that evening after Richards had gone. The first was a simple case of money and the other, perhaps more complicated, was why had Mrs Blatherley decided to split the estate up into small sections. Let's face it, a big estate like that, particularly one dedicated to hunting, would normally be snatched up by any one of several wealthy landowners, all eager to let blood flow on an even larger scale. It didn't make a lot of sense to Ada or me.

'There's only one way to find out, Eddie. I'll ring her up and try to get some more information. However, I think I'll phone Dick first just in case we end up with some more trouble to sort out.'

Dick knew nothing more than we did but suggested that we shouldn't mention her husband unless the matter was brought up by Mrs Blatherley.

'Eddie, I think Dick still feels he has to look out for me. But I suppose he means well. I'll see if I can find Mrs B's number in the telephone book, if I can find the book, that is.'

It was around 8 pm when the phone rang, and surprisingly, it was Richards again. He asked if we had heard a shot nearby around the time that Jenkins was last seen. He said some walkers had heard one and thought it came from around our area.

'Eddie, did you hear a shot the other day?' Ada called out.

'Not that I can recall. It's out of season for shooting, anyway. I'm sure I would have heard it otherwise. Which day? Ask him.'

'He says Tuesday.'

'Is that morning or afternoon?'

'He says forget it. Sergeant Richards, can you find for me Mrs Blatherley's telephone number? It's not in my book. Is it a local number?'

After half an hour, Richards called back and gave Ada the London number of Mrs Blatherley's apartment and bid Ada good luck almost as if he meant it. Ada immediately dialled the number and was cordially answered by the woman at the other end of the line.

'Hello, Ruth Blatherley speaking. Can I help you?' She obviously was used to political inquiries from her response.

'Mrs Blatherley, my name is Ada Gampe. I own a piece of land adjoining your estate on the North York Moors...'

'Ada Gampe ... well, well, well! You know I've been dying to meet you and your companion ever since my husband disappeared. What's his name ... oh, yes, Edward Dew. I don't know too much of your story but I know I need to thank you for your help in ridding me of that dreadful man. Look, I'm going back to the estate at the weekend and I would like us to meet up. Can you come to lunch at the house on, let's say, Saturday at 1 pm?'

Ada agreed and seemed somewhat overcome.

'Well, that was most unexpected. I wonder what she's been told and who's been telling her.'

***

Lunch turned out to be what Ada and I would call dinner by its size, but it lacked the freshness of newly picked garden vegetables that we enjoy. It served its purpose, however, as the background for our conversation.

Ruth Blatherley was very much unlike Ada or me, having been brought up in the luxurious surroundings of the northern foothills of India. She was the daughter of wealthy tea planters and had been surrounded by servants. She was fair-skinned, elegantly dressed and a little younger than Ada and me and was quite glamorous. But two things stood out quite clearly. The first was her innocence or naiveté and the other was the state of her hands. They were spotless, unblemished, her fingers slender and lacking any sign of physical labour. Ada had noticed them, too. But for all that, she was a nice person, polite, but maybe a little too talkative.

'Now, you two have done me a great service in more ways than you can possibly imagine. First of all, I was contacted by a thin young man who gave me his name as Oscar. He informed me that my husband was involved in some very shady business and that I would be wise to keep out of his affairs until all was settled. I decided to come back here for a while, but everything had changed. My husband was already here and the people he had invited to stay were abominable. In reality, I didn't feel safe in the house with them.

'And then there was the smell. It was horrible. Every cupboard in the kitchen was stuffed with dead birds and animals, some lying on shelves, others hanging up with maggots dropping off them onto the floor. It was dreadful. I thought he'd gone mad, and when I asked him why there were so many, all he could say was that he had a lot of entertaining to do. And he did ... and what a crowd!

'God, if you could have seen them. Most of them were from abroad, but there was this atrocious little rat of a man, Wragge his name was, used to be a policeman. I'm sure he never washed his clothes. What with him and the so-called gamekeeper, I just had to leave.

'My husband became so rude as well. It appeared to me that if there was anybody with any decency in them, he would treat them like dirt, but if they were obviously nasty, then he fostered them as if they were his oldest friends. What a nightmare!

'I left one night and thought I'd go off to Paris for a while to get away from him, I was met in London by a woman police officer, plainclothes, Diana something. She took me to an office somewhere near the Tower of London, Crutched Friars I think, and told me that my husband was implicated in the murders of Ernest Dew and his daughter, Marina, and that you, Ada Gampe, had already been attacked by a group of assassins hired by my husband. It all seemed to fit together.

'Then she said that for my own safety, I should go with her to a safe place until the situation was resolved. So what could I do? I went with her. She put me in a very comfortable little cottage in Dorset. She even had my dog kidnapped from the big house and sent down to me and gave me a new name. And that was that! Quite bizarre, but I went along with it as I had little trust in my husband at that point.'

Ada and I just looked at each other and smiled. I thought that I should say something without giving too much away. 'Marina was my niece, you know. I never understood why she was murdered. Have you any ideas?'

Ruth Blatherley was visibly shocked. I could tell that she had no more information than what she had told us. In her own way, she was just another victim of her despicable husband and, of course, she had no idea that he was dead. We chatted for a bit longer until Ada thought it was time to mention the land.

'We understand that you are selling off the estate in plots. We might be interested in buying some small part of it.'

'I am being very choosy as to whom I sell the land. Firstly, I am thoroughly disgusted with all the slaughter that has taken place on the estate. I don't care if the beaters and keepers do complain. I can't believe they can possibly have any self-respect. It's about time they found proper work instead of kowtowing to a bunch of bloodletting toffs. So I will not sell to anyone who wants to use the land for hunting or shooting. I had thought about planting some little plots of woodland here and there, but it's a lot of work and I don't know how much money my husband left in England before he ran off.

'I understand that there is an international warrant out for him for importing cocaine. I found out that Customs and Excise found parcels of it all over London with his name on them. I never knew what kind of man I'd married until that came up. It was hard evidence and I had to believe it. So what have you in mind for my land if I sell some of it to you?'

I knew what I would do, but I left it to Ada to explain her ideas.

'Trees, donkeys, nest boxes for little birds, nest boxes for owls, insect hotels, wildflowers, ponds for frogs, toads and newts, rocks for lizards and a big fence to keep them all safe. And that's just for starters.'

I could see Ruth well up as Ada described our plans. 'Oh my, that's exactly what I want, too! I don't really want money. I want to look out of my windows and see peace around me. Ada, Edward, can we work together on this? What would you say if I turned the estate into a trust run by the three of us with equal shares in the enterprise?'

'It's not quite as simple as that, Ruth. It will need an income, a large income, to work.'

'Well, there's my husband's collection of Chinese and Japanese ivory carvings and his collection of contemporary art. You know, he has three Damian Hirsts in our bedroom and I know he's got a book full of Tracey Emin's private parts. It's on top of his wardrobe. I'd be glad to see the back of that lot and then, of course, there's the portrait. My beloved all dressed up in his hunting gear. What a pompous idiot! I tell you what; we'll burn that one.'

And so the conversation and plans progressed. Ada was amused but not totally convinced that there would be enough income for the initial idea until Ruth mentioned the rest. There were cars and shares in oil, sugar, coffee, and gas and every privatised utility. There would certainly be enough.

***

In the following weeks, staff were hired to labour or write, and the trust became a reality. Volunteers came each week, some to do the planting and others to tend the crops or help build chalets for the workforce. A true environmental enterprise.

Meeting Ruth helped me clear up some of my own problems. I have explained a great deal, but what Ruth let on was that having been so close to the great evil that consumed her husband had changed her. Her blindness of what and who he became was lifted and she became a powerful force for good, the complete opposite of her husband. Ruth was unwilling to continue being Blatherley's victim, and having met Ada, she was able to carry forward the things that she could previously only dream of.

As for me, the idea that Ada impressed upon me was that I could eliminate an evil person and feel justified. Sometimes one might feel the urge to do away with a wrongdoer, but then there is often a dilemma. Is it right to kill an evil person because they deserve to be killed? It's a hard judgement to make before taking the final step.

Religion played no part in my acceptance of what I had done. At St Michael, we were exposed to the teachings of the Bible, and even then I had questions that I dared not ask for fear of seeming dumb or creating controversy. As time went on, I became much more aware of the evil that existed in the world and wondered why such things happened in spite of religious beliefs.

For me, it became more important to do good unto others and be kind until my sense of decency became a target for mean people who took advantage of my vulnerabilities. I never understood that. I decided it was best to stay away from humanity as much as possible and instead interact with nature and the innocent creatures that she nurtured.

With Jenkins, it was clear that he was holding all the cards. He held a gun to me, had just cold-heartedly killed an innocent bird, and was intent on destroying the lives of my dear furry friends. It was clear that he fed on evil, and because of that and the fact that it was either him or me, I judged that he had not earned the right to live.

Then again, Jenkins may have just been a lackey for the depraved wishes of his employers who were probably worse than him in many respects. The fact remains that he had the choice. The kind of people who employed him are like a virus destroying all that is good in the name of amusement.

Really, the government should take steps to eliminate them as they would a disease, but unfortunately, it relies on people like Jenkins to fuel its own fires with rotten meat and decayed bones. And that's the way I see it.

Believe me, when you've seen the quantity of dead animals maimed and left to die by so-called marksmen and hunters as I have, seen their dead bodies writhing from the mass of maggots within them as if they were still alive, you know there is no justification for that kind of behaviour. So Jenkins died and I have absolutely no remorse. Ada killed Blatherley and has no remorse either. It's in the nature of the moment that we believe we did the right things, but, of course, we can never speak of them to anyone.

Obviously, all this will fade into memory and time will bury the whole story, and one day, when my and Ada's time comes, it will become no more than just another story, lost in the pile of a million others.

I'm just glad that Jim Cuttance had a chance to succeed while Dick, Merry, Militant and Edyta and all the others are still ready and waiting for another ominous call from Joseph for assistance to stamp down upon another viper writhing in a nest of corruption. I just hope that when that time comes, we, too, will be ready for his call, provided, of course, that we are not too busy planting trees with Ruth.

Chapter 28

Just when I thought that our story was starting a new chapter, something happened which changed our lives.

One night about three months ago, we heard a movement outside the house, and Ada, being much more alert than me, grabbed a pistol and went to investigate. I fumbled in the drawer for my gun but realised that after cleaning it, I had left it in the barn in its case. I went to the bedroom to find another, and then I heard it. A single shot.

From the window, I could just make out Ada lying on the ground with a figure standing over her pointing a gun at her head, obviously waiting to be sure she was dead. Ada always kept an old, loaded Colt .45 by the bed which I grabbed, and running back to the open window, I aimed and pulled the trigger. The man fell backwards with that single shot.

I was with Ada within seconds. She was still alive but only just. She looked up at me as I knelt down beside her and said in a kind of sobbing voice, 'Oh, my Eddie, I love you. Remember me, won't you?' Then she was gone.

I put my face to hers, my tears blinding me for an instant— and then the rage. It swelled like a whale breaching the waves, and there I was standing over the groaning body of my love's murderer. I held the .45 close to his head and fired round after round until all the chambers were empty, his head almost gone. Still I continued, fierce, full of hatred. I rushed to the barn and took the same pitchfork that had introduced me to Ada and plunged it time and again into the corpse.

Finally, my energy gave way to tears and I staggered indoors carrying the body of my dearest love, laying her gently on the sofa. I sat down beside her, drowning in my own sorrow for hour upon hour. Tiredness overcame me, and I must have fallen asleep until the first call of the blackbird ushered the light of a new dawn.

Sitting beside Ada, I stroked her cold face, held her fingers tightly in mine and wept as I have never wept before. I gently kissed her pale lips time and again, my tears flowing onto her eyelids and trickling down her cheeks as if she, too, was crying.

It was around ten when I called Dick and told him of the shocking events. I had decided to make a run for it, take up my old life again and hide myself away from all human contact. Dick agreed but told me to wait until he arrived.

I had packed up some stuff—provisions, a couple of blankets, a plastic tarp. I took Ada's hat as a memento and as something to wear and waited.

Dick was shocked when he saw what I had done to the murderer and said, 'Eddie, for Christ's sake, what have you done? All I could do was shrug my shoulders and look away.

'Eddie, look, you will need this. It contains information on how to reach me directly. Give me a call in a couple of days. You know they will come for you, don't you? The police first and then the others. Be really vigilant. If the police get you, remember I am your brief and believe me, you will need me. You'd better get going, I'll call the police for Ada. As for the other guy, that's their problem. Go on, go!'

That was exactly what I did, running off like a dog with its tail stuck firmly between its back legs. It was the loneliest time that I ever had, bereft of all that had brought me into the light of day, my most precious Ada, dead, cold and for what?

As I looked around, I realised that I could never go back to living on the moor as I had done. In fact, the idea of survival was no longer there. I had lost everything that meant anything to me. My Ada was gone and I knew of no way to move on from that. The moor, which had once welcomed me, felt hostile, harsh, with a coldness that seeped deep into my spirit.

On the evening of the second day, I decided to call Dick. I had nothing left to live for. There was suddenly no purpose in living any longer.

I went back to the house to talk to the ghost that now haunted my mind, and as I waited for Dick's arrival, I wandered from room to room looking for any sign that Ada was still there. But, of course, she wasn't. There was nothing left except our possessions, hollow echoes of our short history—and now she was gone—forever gone.

Dick was quite late but brought with him a couple of draft papers which needed my signature. I had decided that everything we had was to go to charities—the land, the house, everything that Ada and I had possessed.

'Dick,' I said, 'could you call Diana. I'm going to give myself up and face the consequences. I can't live out there again, not being hunted and with all those memories. It would be too much to bear.'

Dick did as I asked. When Diana arrived, they both tried to talk me out of it, but I just couldn't go on as I was before I met Ada. Diana even said that she could get me out of the country to a safe destination but I declined. I told them, 'For the first time in my life, I had something, someone who cared for me. She was my life and it was taken away from me. There is nothing more to lose. I know what will happen, and I feel that the sooner it takes place the better.' Diana hugged me and said that she understood.

They took me to York where I gave myself up at the central police station. I was arrested and charged with murder along with several other charges and then led to the cell.

As I went, I saw Dick and Diana enter through the doorway, and I knew at least that I wouldn't be mishandled this time. The police can be pretty rough with outcasts, you know, pushing, punching, that sort of thing and worse.

The next morning I was in front of the magistrate. Dick was there to make sure everything was okay and then, being put on remand, I was loaded into a van and taken off to prison to await my trial.

I can barely remember the next few hours. All I had on my mind was a picture of Ada, scenes one after another of our lives together and finally her last words to me as she died in front of me, blood slowly oozing from a bullet wound to her chest and blood trickling from the side of her lips.

Well, I don't think I will be here for too much longer. I have that feeling rooting inside me and Ada's voice calling me to join her. Nothing matters anymore.

The days have passed without me noticing. It is as if time no longer exists. I see other prisoners, hollow-faced, their voices as they speak to me are silent, and I find I do not understand what they are saying to me. And then they turn away.

Ada is with me all the time now. I can feel her drawing my spirit away from my body, and soon I will be with her again. I have noticed one prisoner who watches my every move. He never takes his eyes off me and he carries menace in his face. I sense that he will be my killer. He is just biding his time.

Ruth came to see me this morning. She is a good person. She brought me a cake and some aftershave, not that I will ever use it. But she warned me that the judge who is on my case is an old friend of her 'departed' husband and will probably hand me the longest possible sentence. I think he will be disappointed that he'll never have the chance to try me.

Dick is coming to see me today. I will give him this final part of my diary. He already has the rest which I left at the house. It's almost like giving part of my life away, but at least it will be an epitaph for Ada and me. Thinking about it, we all had some fun and some tragedies, met old friends and made new ones. I shall take those memories with me. I have no regrets except for one ... that Ada and I never had the chance to live out our dreams together. Who knows. Maybe in the next life, things will turn out differently.

Chapter 29

Three days after meeting with Eddie, I received a call from the prison to tell me that Eddie was dead and his body now lay in the prison mortuary. They asked me what I wanted to do with him. They declared that he committed suicide and that's what was stated on the death certificate. Knowing Eddie so well and having read the last of his diary, I knew that this was suspicious. I demanded that the corpse be released to Diana, and I would arrange for an independent postmortem.

Diana and I collected Eddie from the mortuary the following morning. As Eddie was being loaded into the hearse, someone from the prison, who shall remain anonymous, cautiously pushed a note into my hand. I read it only after we had left the vicinity of the prison. The note said, 'He was suffocated. The man who dunnit is gone. Your man was set up for it. The guvnor knew. He let it happen. Two guards helped as well. Somebody got paid for it.'

Sure enough, the postmortem showed bruises on Eddie's wrists and ankles consistent with being firmly held down while he was suffocated, probably with a pillow as there were no marks on his neck. I get the feeling that he knew what was coming and didn't fight it.

Diana arranged for Ada's body to be released since there was no longer any necessity for the police to hold it. Her death certificate stated that she died from misadventure though it was a clear case of murder.

Diana and I were seriously concerned as to how much corruption we were running into since the conspiracy seemed to stretch beyond all imagining. Joseph was quite concerned as well and suggested that he should make the trip, not only for the funeral, but to get a better idea as to who might be involved.

We wanted Ada and Eddie to have a proper send off, and after speaking to the funeral director, it was decided that they should lie together in one coffin facing each other with an arm draped across each other's waists as if in an eternal embrace, the two bound together with a sash of crimson silk. Obviously, it would take more than four pallbearers to carry such a large coffin but that was just a minor problem for us to solve. It didn't seem right to any of us that these two heroes should be placed in a cemetery, so Ruth arranged and got permission from local planning to have them buried at the entrance to the new woodland that they had started to plant.

Eventually, all the plans for the funeral were set. Joseph brought with him Militant and Edyta, Merry and several of the others who wanted to pay their respects. Militant brought with him a seedling from an ancient yew tree which was still growing after a thousand years in a churchyard in the Sussex village of Wilmington. He said, 'This will stand over them for another thousand years.'

When the day came, the coffin, decked in purple and black, was carried on a mobile trestle drawn by two black horses whose hooves were decorated with sapphire blue ribbons. There were no flowers except two white roses carelessly placed upon the covering and whose petals had already fallen. They were lowered gently into the earth as everyone held their breaths. Each took a handful of earth and scattered it upon the box and then the grave digger took up his position and commenced to fill the space.

Ruth led the mourners to her mansion where food and drink was waiting. Everyone was silent. Militant made a toast, Edyta cried, Diana and I held hands as Merry sneaked a sandwich into her mouth piece by piece. Tom sat pensively in a chair drinking a glass of wine.

Eventually Joseph raised his glass. 'Damn the solemnity! Let's be happy that they are together now forever. Come, let's drink to their eternal love and unity. Imagine them a thousand years from now, still bound together with a crimson silk sash. To Ada and Eddie!'

It certainly broke the ice, and the wake commenced in earnest. But again, it was Joseph who clearly was thinking of other things. Revenge was on his mind. I could see it in his eyes.

'Joseph?' I questioned. 'You have something on your mind and I have a pretty good notion as to its source.'

'Yes. I think we are both on the same theme,' he replied. 'Who the devil is behind all this? One thing is for sure. They still want that land or is it just revenge? I can't fathom it. But somebody has to pay for this. If they don't, we could all end up in the ground.

'Look, Dick, I've got a favour to ask. I know Eddie wanted everything to go to various charities but the fact remains that the action seems to be centred around here. Therefore, we need a base to work from if we are agreed to do something about the killing of our dear friends. So what I had in mind is Ada's house. Can we use that?'

'Joseph, that will not be a problem, but who is going to live there and keep everything going?' Neither he nor I had noticed that we had an audience.

'Me!' she said. Needless to say, it was Merry. 'Dick? Have you still got Ada's guns? We're going to need them, aren't we?'

I replied that I had them well hidden but suggested that she should have somebody with her if we agreed to Joseph's idea.

'Oh, don't worry about that. My friend Jean will be with me. I couldn't leave her behind. Besides that, she was a physicist at Porton Down and knows quite a lot about explosive devices. That could come in handy.'

At that point, I thought it necessary to bring Diana, Militant, Edyta and Tom into the picture, but I felt that Ruth was not up to the rough and tumble that might occur. I allowed things to carry on with Merry sworn to secrecy.

As the afternoon wore on, I could see that Ruth was beginning to tire, so I called everyone together and suggested that, because there were still some things to discuss, we should trek down to Ada and Eddie's house for a final discussion. It sounded a bit ominous but everyone agreed.

As the afternoon stayed quite bright with a slight warm breeze blowing in from the south, the walk didn't seem so laborious. As we trekked the same trails that Ada and Eddie had travelled, there was an eerie silence among the group. The leaves seemed to rustle louder, the bird songs sounded almost melancholic; the fallen twigs crackled here and there as small creatures scampered to hide. For the first time, I experienced the wonder of what Ada and Eddie once knew. It touched me beyond measure.

'Well, everybody, here we are, the scene of Ada's murder and Eddie's so-called felony. That is the real reason I got you here. There are certain questions that desperately need answers and that is what I am going to talk about.' It seemed that I had the total attention of everyone.

'Right,' I continued, 'firstly, why was Ada murdered? Secondly, what did the prison governor have to do with Eddie's murder? Thirdly, why was there a false autopsy report of suicide? Fourthly, who do the prison wardens work for? And lastly, is the government involved in any way? We need answers and to get them is going to take a lot of work. So, who among you is interested in participating in this adventure?' The show of hands was encouraging. Everybody was in.

Militant was the first to ask questions. 'Where do we start? It's not going to be possible from Southampton or the Isle of Wight. They're too far away. What about this place? How many bedrooms are there?'

'Two bedrooms only. However, Diana is with me in York, not too far away, and Joseph can stay with me as well. Merry and her friend Jean will take one room. Militant, you and Edyta can take the other. Tom, you can stay with us in York or at the farmhouse. Your choice. Come into the barn, everyone. I have something to show you all.'

I took them to Ada's cellar below the barn. 'This was Ada's secret workshop where she made her bullets, repaired her guns, and created some of her inventions.' The group meandered about the room, surveying Ada's arsenal with wild-eyed amazement.

Diana decided that she had to make a few enquiries and went back to the house with Joseph, who had a few questions of his own. Militant went upstairs to survey the grounds above, and I joined him.

In a contemplative mode, Militant reflected, 'I still can't believe they're gone ... two of the nicest people you could ever meet. I remember back at St Michael, Eddie and I were always targeted for bashings but for different reasons. I was the outspoken rebel and Eddie was the quiet oddball, always kept to himself, I guess as a way to go unnoticed.

'During recess, I'd often see him feeding bits of his lunch to birds or squirrels or stray cats. I figured somehow they could see his kind spirit because they'd land on his hand or boldly walk right up to him. It was amazing to watch. Eventually, we ran away together but somehow lost track of each other. I'll always regret that.'

It was difficult to watch a strapping man get teary-eyed. 'Militant, I understand how you're feeling. What's happened to them is vile and unforgivable but we need to get past this and do what's right by them. We need to honour them by carrying on their work and holding accountable those who committed these heinous acts. The corruption and wanton extermination is endemic and we can't give up and let them prevail and get away with it. Someone is responsible and we need to find out who the puppet master is. And we start now.'

'Right. I'm with you, Dick. Count me in. Let's go.'

Chapter 30

'Echis 390.'

'Basilisk here. I request to speak with Anemone.'

'Your point of entry, Basilisk?'

'SCT 5.'

The society member looked through his roster and confirmed his identity. 'I'll see if she's in.' After a pause, 'Connecting.'

'Well, well, Basilisk. What took you so long?'

'I don't know what you mean but I need an update. Who's in charge now?'

'He goes by the name of Cronym and you can only get to him through me unless he specifically requests an audience with you.'

Basilisk responded, 'Hmm, are you usually there too or do I have to make a special request?'

'Do you have a message I can convey to him?' she said brusquely.

'Right. Tell him that I've been entrenched with Sphinx as an undercover. I'm sure that records of the sordid events and my involvement are accessible to him if he doesn't know about it already. The main targets, Adam and Eve, have been eliminated. However, the group is still active and highly motivated to finish what they started. We stand to lose an enormous amount of wealth if we just let them get on with it.'

Anemone's keyboard could be heard clicking as he spoke. 'Anything else?'

'Tell him that I'm still in a position to stop them but will need Blatherley's list of hitmen to assist me. If he's onboard, he can reach me at this number for a meeting.'

'I'll get this to him straightaway. Good luck, Basilisk.'

He hung up the phone, and deep in thought, absentmindedly fingered the viper's opal eyes on his silver wristlet.

About the Author

Barry Harden was born and raised in the vibrant streets of North Harrow, London. His storytelling reflects the rich tapestry of his upbringing, where he developed a keen eye for social dynamics and a deep appreciation for the world's wonders. In his memoir, *Throwaway*, he candidly reveals the frayed tapestry of his own life, complemented by four fiction novels that explore the full spectrum of human experiences, from the realms of political intrigue to the fantastical. With two books of poetry that resonate with lyrical Gothic symbolism and two collections of satirical short stories, Harden's creative range knows no bounds.

But beneath the enthralling intrigue, adventures and Gothic motifs lie profound sociopolitical perspectives that inspire reflection. And when it comes to satire, Harden's wit is a scalpel that cuts through the absurdities of our world, revealing uncomfortable truths with a humorous twist. His stories are a testament to his unwavering commitment to storytelling and his unyielding belief in the power of words to change the world.

A dedicated proponent of animal rights and environmental protection, Harden's affinity for these causes often seeps into his writing. He has lived in the south of France where for two decades he ran a sanctuary for wayward cats. Harden now calls the sunny shores of Florida home.

From the Author

Thank you for purchasing *Ada & Eddie*. I genuinely hope that your reading experience of this book was as enriching as my experience writing it. If you have a moment to spare, I would greatly appreciate it if you could share your thoughts about the book on your preferred online platform for reviews. Additionally, if you're interested in staying updated on my upcoming works, recent blog posts, or joining a community of fellow readers, please visit my website where you can find news about forthcoming projects and sign up for my newsletter. Your support and feedback mean a lot to me. https://www.barryhardenauthor.com.

Sincerely,
Barry Harden

ROUNDFIRE
BOOKS

FICTION

Put simply, we publish great stories. Whether it's literary or popular, a gentle tale or a pulsating thriller, the connecting theme in all Roundfire fiction titles is that once you pick them up you won't want to put them down.
If you have enjoyed this book, why not tell other readers by posting a review on your preferred book site.

The Cause
Roderick Vincent
The second American Revolution will be a
fire lit from an internal spark.
Paperback: 978-1-78279-763-0 ebook: 978-1-78279-762-3

Don't Drink and Fly
The Story of Bernice O'Hanlon: Part One
Cathie Devitt
Bernice is a witch living in Glasgow. She loses her way
in her life and wanders off the beaten track looking for the
garden of enlightenment.
Paperback: 978-1-78279-016-7 ebook: 978-1-78279-015-0

Gag
Melissa Unger
One rainy afternoon in a Brooklyn diner, Peter Howland
punctures an egg with his fork. Repulsed, Peter pushes
the plate away and never eats again.
Paperback: 978-1-78279-564-3 ebook: 978-1-78279-563-6

The Master Yeshua
The Undiscovered Gospel of Joseph
Joyce Luck
Jesus is not who you think he is. The year is 75 CE. Joseph
ben Jude is frail and ailing, but he has a prophecy to fulfil ...
Paperback: 978-1-78279-974-0 ebook: 978-1-78279-975-7

On the Far Side, There's a Boy
Paula Coston

Martine Haslett, a thirty-something 1980s woman, plays hard on the fringes of the London drag club scene until one night which prompts her to sign up to a charity. She writes to a young Sri Lankan boy, with consequences far and long.
Paperback: 978-1-78279-574-2 ebook: 978-1-78279-573-5

Tuareg
Alberto Vazquez-Figueroa

With over 5 million copies sold worldwide, *Tuareg* is a classic adventure story from best-selling author Alberto Vazquez-Figueroa, about honour, revenge and a clash of cultures.
Paperback: 978-1-84694-192-4

Readers of ebooks can buy or view any of these bestsellers by clicking on the live link in the title. Most titles are published in paperback and as an ebook. Paperbacks are available in traditional bookshops. Both print and ebook formats are available online.

Find more titles and sign up to our readers' newsletter, visit:
www.collectiveinkbooks.com/fiction